THE

*Last Beach
Bungalow*

THE

Last Beach Bungalow

JENNIE NASH

BERKLEY BOOKS, NEW YORK

THE BERKLEY PUBLISHING GROUP
Published by the Penguin Group
Penguin Group (USA) Inc.
375 Hudson Street, New York, New York 10014, USA

Penguin Group (Canada), 90 Eglinton Avenue East, Suite 700, Toronto, Ontario M4P 2Y3, Canada
(a division of Pearson Penguin Canada Inc.)
Penguin Books Ltd., 80 Strand, London WC2R 0RL, England
Penguin Group Ireland, 25 St. Stephen's Green, Dublin 2, Ireland (a division of Penguin Books Ltd.)
Penguin Group (Australia), 250 Camberwell Road, Camberwell, Victoria 3124, Australia
(a division of Pearson Australia Group Pty. Ltd.)
Penguin Books India Pvt. Ltd., 11 Community Centre, Panchsheel Park, New Delhi—110 017, India
Penguin Group (NZ), 67 Apollo Drive, Rosedale, North Shore 0632, New Zealand
(a division of Pearson New Zealand Ltd.)
Penguin Books (South Africa) (Pty.) Ltd., 24 Sturdee Avenue, Rosebank, Johannesburg 2196,
South Africa

Penguin Books Ltd., Registered Offices: 80 Strand, London WC2R 0RL, England

This is a work of fiction. Names, characters, places, and incidents either are the product of the author's
imagination or are used fictitiously, and any resemblance to actual persons, living or dead, business
establishments, events or locales is entirely coincidental. The publisher does not have any control over
and does not assume any responsibility for author or third-party websites or their content.

Copyright © 2008 by Jennie Nash
Readers Guide copyright © 2008 by Jennie Nash
Cover design by Rita Frangie
Cover photo by La Coppola-Meier / Photonica / Getty
Book design by Tiffany Estreicher

All rights reserved.
No part of this book may be reproduced, scanned, or distributed in any printed or electronic form with-
out permission. Please do not participate in or encourage piracy of copyrighted materials in violation
of the author's rights. Purchase only authorized editions.
BERKLEY® is a registered trademark of Penguin Group (USA) Inc.
The "B" design is a trademark belonging to Penguin Group (USA) Inc.

PRINTING HISTORY
Berkley trade paperback edition / February 2008

Library of Congress Cataloging-in-Publication Data

Nash, Jennie, 1964-
    The last beach bungalow / Jennie Nash.—Berkley trade paperback ed.
       p. cm.
    ISBN 978-0-425-21927-0 (pbk.)
    1. Dwellings—Psychological aspects—Fiction.   2. Psychological fiction.   I. Title.

PS3614.A73L37 2008
813'.6—dc22

                                                                        2007024724

PRINTED IN THE UNITED STATES OF AMERICA

10   9   8   7   6   5   4   3   2

*Locatedness is not a science of the ground,
but of some quality within us.*
—RICHARD FORD

For Rob
Home is where you are.

ACKNOWLEDGMENTS

The idea for this book came to me in a flash on a yellow school bus, and a whole busload of friends and associates have helped me bring it to life. Kristine Breese, my writing soulmate, read every single page of every single draft and made it better each time through her intelligence, spirit and generosity. Lisa Edmondson, friend and guru, guided me at a critical moment to see what the flash on the bus was really all about. Beth Kephart, novelist and pen pal, provided constant and poetic long-distance encouragement. My husband, Rob, gave me a living, breathing model of a loving husband. My children, Carlyn and Emily, talked about my characters at the dinner table as if they were real people, which helped me come to see them that way, too. My sister, Laura, helped me with the music and other truths. My friends Barbara Abercrombie, Danny Brassell, Patti Goldenson, Denise Honaker, Lori Logan, Bridget O'Brian (who has been reading my work with keen insight for

ACKNOWLEDGMENTS

more than two decades!), Trisha Rappaport, and Susan Sawyer read and commented on various drafts. Faye Bender, my literary agent, guided me through a seamless genre switch and made an inspired match. Jackie Cantor, my editor, cried in all the right places (and in front of all the right people!), saw more in my work than I ever knew was there, and welcomed me into a hardworking team of professionals that included assistant Carolyn Morrisroe, cover designer Rita Frangie, copyeditor Denise Barricklow, and publicist Catherine Milne. Heartfelt thanks to you all!

THE

Last Beach Bungalow

WEDNESDAY

There's something oddly comforting about doctors' waiting rooms. The art on the walls is always soothing, the receptionist at the desk is always cheerful, people's voices are hushed and almost reverent, and the air is infused with the promising smell of soap, as if, behind the door, it's not just people's bodies that are being healed, but their lives that are being swept clean of anything that smacks of deficiency or decay. I couldn't in a million years have become a doctor myself, since I lack two essential qualifications—namely a benign attitude toward blood and an ability to drum up compassion for strangers who, more often than not, bring their problems upon themselves. But in a strange way, my chosen field shares some of the same principles with the ancient art of healing. I'm a magazine writer, a freelancer—one of those people who brings you monthly promises of a thin waist, shining hair, fabulous shoes, an effortless vacation and a husband who happily does the dishes. I, too, operate on a faith that just about anything can be made better.

I shuffled through the magazines on the waiting room table and grabbed a two-year-old *Metropolitan Home.* I recognized it as an issue that contained an article I'd done on the merits of cork flooring, which, I had learned, is actually a renewable resource. It's made from the bark of trees, so during harvest the trees aren't damaged. As a floor, cork is warm and forgiving. It also has the unusual property of being mold resistant, which, in the foggy beach cities of Los Angeles, is a definite plus.

I read the words I'd written with a cool satisfaction, then tossed *Metropolitan Home* back on the pile and picked up the new issue of *Town & Country*. A flock of subscription and perfume cards fluttered onto my lap. I picked them up and had just started scanning the table of contents when someone called my name.

"April Newton?" a woman sang, with a slight rise at the end of my last name, as if questioning whether I was still there and had not, in fact, given up on getting my turn in the inner sanctum. I smiled to indicate that I was, indeed, April Newton. I stood and kept the magazine with me as I grabbed my purse and followed the woman down the hall.

I followed her past the large tropical fish tank and noticed that she was wearing soft pink scrubs that matched the soft pink walls. We walked down the hallway, which was hung with large black-and-white close-ups of roses and tulips, and into a dressing room with muted lighting. "Everything off but your panties," the woman said. "Robe opens to the front. Put your clothes in one of the lockers and keep the key in your robe pocket."

I fought the urge to interrogate this woman the way I might if I had been sent to interview her on a piece about the new customer-service features of breast care facilities around the country. *How many times,* I would ask, *do you estimate you've given those instructions? Do you ever just know, by their eyes or the way they hold their shoulders, that some women already know what to do? That they have, in fact, heard those instructions so many times that it sounds to them now like a poem or the lyrics to an old song? That they would rather dispense with the robe altogether, knowing that what they've come here to do is bare their bodies and their souls?*

"Thank you," I said, in response to her speech about clothing protocol.

I went to unzip my jeans and noticed that the zipper was already halfway down. This had been happening with some frequency lately and more than anything else, it surprised me. I had become thick around the middle. After so many years paying so much attention to my body—to how fit it was, how healthy, how resilient, how balanced—I had become thick around the middle without even realizing that it had happened. I took off my pants, pulled off my sweater, unhooked my bra—which had turned a kind of murky gray, speckled with little balls of pilled elastic—wrapped myself in a thick terry cloth robe and took the *Town & Country* into the inner waiting room.

It was a lounge like a spa. There was a pitcher of ice water and lemon on the side table, along with fresh brewed tea and a tray of shortbread cookies. Norah Jones was being piped in through speakers in the ceiling. I took a seat in a plush armchair. There was only one other woman in the waiting room with me, a woman about my age with hair even more red than mine and what appeared to be an immunity to the charms of women's magazines. She sat in her own armchair on the other side of the low coffee table, with her arms crossed primly in her lap. My guess was that she'd never had a mammogram, and for a split second, I thought about breezily making such a guess. "First time?" I might say, as if coming to an appointment whose sole purpose was to determine whether or not you had cancer was something you could get used to.

I opened the *Town & Country* again. It was a magazine I'd never written for, which presented a kind of puzzle for me to solve. What was their style? How did they structure their pages? I turned to the wedding section and read the names of a couple who frolicked in the water off Martha's Vineyard and another who posed on a wide swath of grass in Ireland, a long-haired setter sitting steadfastly by the groom. I flipped again to a section in the feature well that was entirely about sex. *Town & Country* sex.

The main feature was a long his-and-hers article by a couple who had gone on a $6,000 sex therapy retreat at the Miraval Resort & Spa in Arizona. I immediately wondered how the piece had been assigned. How had the editors known that the writer and her spouse would be game for such an intimate outing? Or had the writers decided to go to the spa, then pitched the piece and gotten their weeklong romp in the desert covered as a business expense? I scanned the wife's section. She quoted one of the sex therapists, who explained that their retreat was designed for couples who were in love, but who had, due to time and the pressures of modern life, lost intimacy. In his section, the man talked mostly about the concept of homework. Sex homework. And he was talking about how much fun it was to be told to do—or not to do—various things in bed with his wife.

"For homework the first night," he wrote, "we were told that if we had intercourse, we would get an F."

For the past nine months, Rick and I had been sleeping in a small double bed in a rented efficiency apartment while workers tore the roof off our ranch house, ripped out the walls, leveled the beams, and then poured a foundation so they could build it all back again—bigger, better, more sleek and modern. Our fifteen-year-old daughter, Jackie, slept three feet from us on the other side of a paper-thin wall, and most nights she didn't go to sleep until two or three hours after I did. I could count on one hand the number of times Rick and I had had sex in those nine months, and all of those times were soon after we moved. We had come to some sort of tacit agreement that our kisses would be chaste, our hands would not roam from the cool zones on our bodies and our eyes would not lock with meaning. It was amazing how much room there could be in a double bed. There was room to roll over, room to spread out, room enough to read and sleep and not once do anything that might be construed as an invitation to intimacy.

I read the words in the article again: "For homework

the first night, we were told that if we had intercourse, we would get an F. My naked wife was to sit in my lap and gaze into my eyes, but there was to be no intercourse. The idea was to connect on a deeper level—to feel the sacredness of sharing our bodies."

I looked up, flushed. The woman with red hair was staring at her hands. At any moment, someone could step in the doorway and call my name. I would have to leave the magazine on the table and wouldn't know what happened to the couple in Arizona. I wouldn't know if they had succeeded at their homework assignment and drawn closer in body and soul, or if they had failed miserably and fallen on each other like hungry animals. I could go to the bookstore and buy this issue of *Town & Country*. Within ten minutes of our apartment, there was both a Borders and a Barnes & Noble, each featuring hundreds of magazine titles just inside their front doors. I knew my way around the aisles as well as if I had stocked them myself, placing stacks of magazines on the rack every week and every month, breathing in their glossy dust, their glittering promise. I could put my hands on that *Town & Country* issue within seconds.

But I knew I wouldn't make a special trip to find out what happened to the couple in Arizona. It would be just one more thing I didn't have time to do.

When a magazine is perfect-bound, like a book, you can rip out pages without a single tear. The trick is to make sure you grab a whole folio—the little bundle of pages that are bound together. When the woman with red hair turned to look at the photographs on the wall, I paged through the sex feature, grasped the pages near the spine of the magazine and ripped them out as quickly and as quietly as I could. The sound shattered the silence of the waiting room like thunder. The woman snapped her head back and gaped at me, but I pretended as if tearing pages from waiting room magazines was a perfectly acceptable practice. I slipped the pages into my robe pocket and reached for a glass of lemon water.

The red-haired woman cleared her throat. "Those magazines are here for everyone's pleasure," she said, not unkindly. I imagined that she was a fourth-grade teacher. She probably said words, or words like these, several dozen times a day to fourth-grade hooligans in the library.

I smiled at her, as if I was pleased that she had appointed herself citizen-watchdog of the doctor's waiting room. "Oh," I said coolly, "it was a subscription ad. I'm going to subscribe. It's a great magazine, *Town & Country*. I don't normally think of it as a magazine of much substance, but there's some solid stuff in there."

She narrowed her brows slightly. They were red, just like her hair. "I'm sorry," she said. "It wasn't my place to say anything. It's just that the reason I'm here is a magazine article."

"Breast self-exam?" I asked. I'd written a dozen such articles myself—about how you should mark your calendar, set aside a full ten minutes, be absolutely methodical in your circular motions around the breast. I never did any of those things myself and, in fact, my doctor told me that only a tiny percentage of women discover cancer in that way.

"No, actually," she said. "It was an article on dating. On how you should look for a man the same way you look for a job. I made a list of attributes I was searching for, and good health was at the top of the list."

"How did that lead you here?" I asked.

"The magazine said that if I wanted to attract someone who made his health a priority, I should make my health a priority, too."

"Smart," I said, although the idea of project management for intimate relationships seemed pretty creepy to me. I had met Rick when I was helping to build a playground at the school where I was teaching. He had designed it, and presumably it was his fault that there was a number ten nail lying in the dirt when I climbed off the scaffolding. The nail went through the sole of my shoe, and before I could even scream, he had pulled the nail out, slapped on antiseptic, bandaged my foot and sent me with one of the other teachers for a tetanus shot.

"We'll see," the red-haired woman said. "I've actually never had a mammogram. I'm a little nervous."

"Ah," I said.

"Have you?"

A pink-clad assistant appeared in the doorway. "April Newton?" she asked.

I got up and went to the doorway. As I passed the red-haired woman, I leaned toward her and gave her my answer. "I've had a few," I said. "It's nothing."

I followed the assistant into the room with the machine. "The technician will be with you shortly," she said, setting my file down on the counter near the sink.

The moment the door closed, I took out the juicy sex article and carefully read the husband's part of the story. When I was done, I bit my lip. I looked out the window, where I could see the tops of three palm trees swaying in the wind and five black birds perched on an electrical wire. I sniffed, thinking I could stop the tears from forming, but my throat was already itching; I had no chance. A teardrop splashed on *Town & Country*.

There was a knock on the door, which flung open as a third woman in soft pink scrubs came blazing into the room. "How are you today?" she called out cheerfully, then took one look at my tear-stained face and picked up my chart. She quickly scanned it. She lowered her voice and said, "Five years is always the hardest."

I shoved the article back into my robe pocket and wiped my eyes with the back of my hand. "No, no," I said, and shook my head. How could I tell this person that it wasn't cancer, exactly, that had me crying? It wasn't the fact that I was moments away from reaching the coveted five-year cancer-free milestone, which, as any good reader of women's magazines knows, is the point at which you revert to having the same risk as any other female of the species. It was the fact that my husband and I would get an A if we were given a homework assignment that had to do with refraining from intercourse. We would be brought up to the front of the class and held up as a model of restraint. Yet just five years before, when our lives had been filled with pathology reports and blood counts, the lurching rhythms of chemotherapy and the endless waiting for test results, Rick and I had been closer than we'd ever been in our lives. We couldn't pass each other without hugging, we couldn't look at each other without meaning. We held hands in the car, we sat thigh-to-thigh whenever we went to a restaurant. It was blasphemous to even form the thought, but I missed those days.

I reached up and pressed my hands to my eye sockets to stop the tears. "I'm sorry," I said, gulping air.

"There's no need to be sorry," she said. "But I need you to be able to hold your breath to get a good picture. Shall I give you a little time?"

"That's OK," I said, shaking my head. "I'll be fine."
I took a deep breath and willed myself to calm down.
I forced the air out of my lungs, stood up and walked
over to the X-ray machine. I dropped the robe from one
shoulder and moved in close to the glass plates. The
technician grabbed my left breast, the real one. Her
hands were freezing. She asked me to scoot closer, and I
leaned toward the machine as if it were a dance partner
who would support my weight and whisk me around
the room. I leaned toward the machine like I loved it,
like it had saved my life.

"Don't move," the technician ordered, as she cranked
the plates together, but I tightly curled my toes in a tiny
act of defiance.

When she was done taking pictures, the technician
asked me to wait in the room while the slides were devel-
oped. "At five years, you're still diagnostic," she explained,
from the doorway. "The radiologist reads it while you're
still in the building. Next year, you'll be screening and
you'll have to wait for the mail like everyone else."

As I sat there waiting, I forgot all about the steamy
reading material in the pocket of my robe. I imagined

what would happen if the technician came back and said she needed to take a few more slides. My heart would start pounding; I'd feel it in my throat. Adrenaline would pump through my body, sending me into a state somewhere oddly close to giddy. She'd take one picture, then two, three and then four. She'd leave for an ominous length of time, then come back and try to tell me the X-rays were fuzzy. Off-kilter. She'd need to do a few more. I'd nod, bare my breast again, hold my breath, knowing without anyone needing to say anything that the cancer was back.

And then what? I'd call Rick. "I'm sorry," I'd say. Sorry that he'd have to go through it again. Sorry that he'd had to go through it before. Sorry that we weren't any better for our brush with mortality—and closer, any happier. Sorry that I'd lost a breast and lost any desire to turn to him in the middle of the night, in the middle of a bed, in an apartment we were renting while we built a house that was supposed to be the place where we'd live for the rest of our lives.

The technician breezed back in and told me everything looked fine. She held my chart in her hands and paused before she slipped out the door again. "Five years," she said. "Congratulations."

"Thank you," I said, and even though she had disappeared from view, I added, "Happy Holidays."

～

I have a friend who has leukemia who has never once been to any cancer-related event in which you have to wear a hat or T-shirt that identifies you as a survivor. She refuses. "You can't be a survivor if you've still got it," she explains. "And I'll always have it." It, of course, being the insidious cells that move and morph within her blood. It, being a thing that saps energy and demands constant vigilance. She pisses me off. *Go to the damn walk,* I want to yell, *wear the damn T-shirt.* This woman who takes chemo the way most of us take multivitamins, throws up with shocking regularity, and has, of late, started to fall because her feet are numb from pain relievers, also volunteers at her nephew's elementary school, coaches a swim team which demands that she stand on a freezing cold pool deck five out of seven nights every week, and, for a regular job, is in charge of our city's youth sports leagues, which means that she is in constant and intimate contact with the most demanding, irrational, frightened and misguided parents in America. And she's not a survivor?

I have another friend who had ovarian cancer when she was just twenty years old. Her father was a surgeon and he stood over her in the operating room when they cut her open and removed her uterus and ovaries. He stood there, inspecting every bit of tissue, making the doctors take their time, making them take out each cell. She's nearing sixty years old, and when people who know anything about ovarian cancer hear that she has lived as long as she has and as well as she has, they practically fall to their knees in awe. But there are no special hats for her to wear, no special pins or special slogans. There are no T-shirts and marches, no lunches in hotel ballrooms with gift bags and speeches. She shrugs when I ask her if she resents it. "I'm alive," she says. "I have no reason to resent anything."

I got in my car and made myself sit there and look at the sunlight and the red Volvo next to me and the

old couple making their way across the parking lot—
he with a walker, she with a cane. I took a deep breath
and thought about giving thanks, but it was exactly
like trying to remember a word you're sure you know
but can't bring to mind. I just couldn't do it. God didn't
make sense anymore. There were people in the Middle
East who were blowing themselves up in the name of
one God, whom they claimed to be almighty. We had
a president who was retaliating in the name of another
God, whom he claimed to be almighty, too. In my
own church—the church of my childhood, of Sunday
mornings and patent leather shoes—people were lock-
ing each other out of sanctuaries over an argument
about how much God loved or didn't love gay people,
because, I presumed, they wanted God to be almighty
for just them alone. The selfish drama of the deity even
played itself out in our apartment complex. Most of the
residents were homeowners in the middle of remodels,
corporate executives in the middle of relocations or first
wives in the middle of divorces, but on the floor below
ours, a Christian rock musician spent his days in a studio
singing praises to God. At night he would sometimes

4241210

shout at his wife with such violence that someone would invariably call the police, and when the police came, the Christian rock band singer would yell for the fucking nigger to mind his own business. I believed there was an unseen force of goodness in the world, something at the center that held it all together and made it all come into being in the first place, but claiming a proprietary personal relationship with God—even one in which I could simply give thanks—had come to seem like an act of folly.

I called Rick on my cell phone. He answered on the first ring. "Hey," he said, his voice as tight as a coiled spring.

"It was all clear," I said.

"Oh, that's great, April," he said. "That's really great."

There was an awkward split second of silence. I leaped into it. "It's been five years this week," I said, as if the thought had only just occurred to me as I sat there in the December sun.

"Has it?" Rick asked. "I guess I've always counted from the day of the surgery, not the day of diagnosis."

This made perfect sense—and if my husband is

known for anything, it's for making perfect sense. You count five years from the day when you could reasonably say the cancer was gone from your body, which in my case was December 10, 1999. But how can you ever really be sure? None of us can ever really be sure. In my mind, there was a day when cancer was just a word—a word I could write about in a magazine, or talk about at dinner—and the next day, the day of diagnosis, it was a reality that had the potential of defining my entire life because it had the potential of ending it. That was the day that mattered to me. And now that I had reached five years, maybe I couldn't say that I had survived, exactly, but maybe I could say that cancer could now be nothing again. Just a word, something that had happened to me once upon a time, a story in the past.

"I was thinking maybe we could have lunch," I said.

"I'm over at the house with Ruben," he said. "We're still wrestling with the backsplash tile. I think we're going to go ahead and build out the wall behind the stove. It's a hassle, but it's the only way to make it plumb. You want to come see if you like the height of the hood?"

The hood that was going over the range in our new

house was Italian. It was an arc of glass and steel, a piece of sculpture, really, that would draw the eye from the family room. We had pendant lights to hang over the central island that mimicked the arch of the range hood. The lights would be reflected in the granite of the island, a spectacular slab of terra-cotta red. Finding these things—the hood, the lights, the stone, the tile, the flooring, the molding and the perfect shade of white paint—had consumed our limited leisure time for the past two years. Instead of lunch, we looked at tile. Instead of sex, we searched together for a range hood.

"Sure," I said, "I could stop and get Subway."

"Great," he said. "See you in a few."

There was no one in line at Subway, though the restaurant was full. A young girl with her hair pulled back in a neat ponytail asked me what I'd like. I scanned the menu, and my eye caught on the descriptions of the platters they offered for holiday catering. You could get a selection of small sandwiches that could feed twenty, plus chips and soda. The signs suggested that this would be an easy way to host an office party, or to entertain guests during New Year's football games. I could have a party to celebrate the fact that I had reached my five-year cancer-free anniversary. I could serve all my friends roast beef and turkey to thank them for how much they'd helped me, for how they'd brought lasagna to our house, picked up Jackie to take her to volleyball practice and sent flowers, cards and soft slippers for me to wear in the hospital.

"Ma'am?" the girl behind the counter asked. There were now three people in line behind me, looking at their watches, glaring at me.

"Oh, I'm sorry," I said. "I'll take three turkey and cheese on sourdough."

"Mustard and mayo?" she asked.

"Yes, thanks," I said.

"Would you like drinks and chips with those?"

"Yes, please," I said, and as she told me the total, my eyes started to tear up again. I closed my eyes and pressed my hand to my lips to keep from weeping out loud. I would get a turkey on sourdough, a Diet Coke and some Lays potato chips to eat on the gleaming granite counter in the middle of my new kitchen. That's how I would celebrate this milestone—with a fast-food meal in a house that my husband had designed and built after my diagnosis because he thought it was what I wanted.

"Ma'am?" the girl asked. I was now crying. I was standing in line at Subway at lunchtime, and I was crying.

"Are you OK?" the woman in line behind me asked. She was wearing black pumps. That's all I could see of her as she grabbed a napkin off the counter and handed it to me. The shoes had pointy toes and a white strap that curved over the top of the foot and ended at a button on the other side. The stitching was black on white and white on black. They were like saddle shoes all grown up and gone to town.

"Why don't you go ahead," I said, and stepped aside. I turned to sit down on a red plastic chair by the door. I was like a child who couldn't get control of her own body. A minute went by, maybe two. The woman in pumps came over and squatted in front of me. She was wearing a black suit with a pencil skirt that had a rim of knife pleats at the hem and a jacket that nipped in at her waist—not the easiest outfit to squat in. She put her hand on my knee, which I thought was incredibly presumptuous and incredibly kind at the same time.

"Is there something I can help you with?" she asked.

"Those are great shoes," I said.

She looked completely unfazed. "They're Kate Spade," she said.

I nodded. I'd written a piece for *Inc.* about Kate Spade many years ago, before I had a child and before Kate got into shoes and dinnerware. I'd sat down to lunch with her at Shutters in Santa Monica and we'd had a great conversation about women's entrepreneurial spirit. We joked about the hippie purse of the woman at the table next to us. I was young, and I was certain that we had bonded in some profound way—that Kate Spade was going to be my friend. I sent her a thank-you note that referenced the joke we'd shared, included my phone number and never heard from her again.

I lifted my eyes to look at the woman in the black suit. She looked smart; Armenian, possibly. She was probably a lawyer who came home at the end of the day and threw together fabulous dinners with lamb and mint. "Have you ever left a pair of shoes behind in a store," I asked, "because you didn't think you needed them or you thought they were too expensive and then one day, years later, they pop into your head—the exact color and shape and even their price—and you think, why didn't I buy those shoes? Why didn't I bring them home?"

The black-suited woman nodded. "It happened to me with a pair of Frye boots in college. Remember Frye boots?"

"Absolutely," I said. "That's what happened to me today, only it wasn't shoes I left behind." She didn't say anything, just squatted there waiting for me to explain. "What I forgot was how to celebrate that I'm alive."

I drove with my sandwiches along the beach, dipped down into the grove of eucalyptus that lined the creek near Malaga Cove, and then climbed up into the hills. The whole of the Los Angeles basin opened up in my rearview mirror. From here, on a clear day, you could see each building of downtown and Century City, the Getty Museum on the very far side of the valley and even the Hollywood sign, if you knew where to look. Our house—which was one of only five houses on the cul-de-sac on the ridge—had a view that looked out the opposite direction, south toward Catalina Island. We could stand in our master bedroom and watch the giant car carriers steaming toward Long Beach Harbor. We could see the sailboats as they made their way up and down the channel. And with a telescope, in winter, we could spot gray whales migrating south to the warm waters of Mexico. It was all water all the time from almost every room of the house. It astonished me every time I saw it.

I pulled into the driveway, got out of the car, walked past the Porta Potti, up the front path—and suddenly felt as if I'd run into a wall of ice. I could hear hammering inside, could see a guy on a ladder fiddling with the outdoor lights, but I couldn't move. Someone yelled something in Spanish, and Rick came to the front door.

"Hey!" he said. He leaped down the front steps and kissed me on the cheek. "Are you OK?" he asked, stepping back from me. "You look like you've seen a ghost."

The ghost of the woman I wanted to be was just inside that door. Her spirit was there, enjoying the view. Her husband's spirit was there, too—the spirit of the man who'd designed and built this house for a wife he hoped wouldn't die. I'd always believed that houses could be haunted. I swore to my mother when I was four years old that there was a ghost who lived in my closet—a friendly ghost who kept the monsters away—but she told me to stop making things up and just go to sleep. Every time I tried to tell her about this wonderful thing, this thing that kept me safe and made me happy, that's what she said: stop making things up and just go to sleep. We only lived in that house a couple of years, but I never forgot the feeling of that ghost.

After my grandmother died, I looked forward to returning to her lakeside cottage in New Hampshire to see if she'd haunt it in the same way. She'd been such a comfort in real life, a woman who taught me to play the piano, who introduced me to Willa Cather and who seemed to understand my mother's sadness in a way I never could. I expected her to be a comfort in death, too. While the adults scurried through her house in a frenzy of sorting and packing, I sat in front of the old stone fireplace, squeezed my eyes shut and convinced myself I could feel my grandmother's presence.

"I feel her here," I said to my mom, but all she said in return was that I should stop daydreaming and help pack up the books.

With so much experience feeling the presence of ghosts who made me comfortable, I didn't think much about the other kind until I got to college. There was an old house next to the church where we used to perform choral concerts—a shingled house with gables and a weather vane. All the kids insisted it was haunted by an old president of the college who had been poisoned by his wife. I used to look at the dark windows of that dark house and think—yes, some evil spirit surely resides there. There was something about the house, even from the outside, that gave me the creeps. I never asserted my conviction about the house being haunted, however, for fear that someone would tell me to stop making things up.

I handed Rick the Subway bag. "What would you say if I said I *had* seen a ghost?" I asked.

"Well, that you're nuts," Rick said.

That night, in the apartment, I lay wide awake as Rick snored beside me. I watched the minutes tick by on the clock and listened to the noises of the night. It was 2:00 A.M., but somewhere in the building someone was taking a shower, someone slammed a door, a car started in the parking lot. It was too late to take Ambien or even Benadryl. I would wake up in the morning as groggy as if I'd been drunk, and I needed to hit the ground running first thing. I had to pick paint colors for the master bath. I had to research an article on lingerie. At three o'clock Jackie had a volleyball game. It would be better not to sleep than to slog through the day on drugs.

"Rick?" I said. He kept snoring. It sounded exactly like a lawnmower. It was amazing that he didn't wake himself up. Had he stopped snoring and replied, I was going to mention the bottle of champagne that we had on top of the refrigerator. One of his clients had given it to him upon completion of their house six months ago. We both knew better than to store a nice bottle of champagne on top of the refrigerator where it was hot, but there was no room in the small refrigerator and nowhere else to put it in the tiny apartment kitchen. There were baking pans stored in the oven and cereal lined up on top of the microwave. I had measuring cups in a cardboard box in the bottom of the broom closet, and every time I needed to measure something, I had to waltz with the broom and wrestle with the vacuum cleaner.

What I would say to Rick was that I thought we should toast five years. Right then, in the middle of the night. We should pop the cork and drink in bed. I could climb into his lap and take off the men's-style button-down pajamas I'd adopted during my season of surgeries, when putting anything on over my head was unthinkable. I would unbutton the buttons slowly, while gazing into his eyes, let the top drop behind me like a stripper, and I would explain that we had a homework assignment.

I looked again at Rick. He was a beautiful man, with a thick head of curly hair, and the compact body of a man who, even at the age of forty-five, thinks nothing of playing an hour-long game of volleyball in the sand or getting up at dawn to surf the big winter swells. He was lying flat on his back. I slipped my hands under his shoulder and shoved as hard as I could.

"You're snoring!" I yelled.

He turned over and kept on sleeping.

I eventually went to sleep, too. I dreamed about being in a house on fire. It was our house—mine and Rick's and Jackie's—but it wasn't any house I actually knew. The fire was going to consume the house—it was big and bad, with thick black smoke, and it had already drawn several screaming fire trucks to the street out front—but I had the sense in my dream the way you sometimes do of time standing still. I had time to collect our wedding photos and time to get Jackie's entire stuffed animal collection and her volleyball trophies. I methodically went around to each of the rooms—ours, but not ours—collecting the things that were important to us. Nothing was left behind. There was no rushing or worrying. I got out with everything I needed, and I consciously left everything else to burn.

THURSDAY

The next morning after Jackie left for school I had to go back to the house. There were four shades of beige and three shades of blue painted in big swatches on the walls of the master bath, and Rick needed me to choose one by noon. I parked the car and managed to make my way through the front door and up the stairs, but there was no denying that same cold feeling of despair. I sat on the toilet to keep myself from bolting out of there. It was a fabulous room, huge and mirrored, with a shower big enough for a party. A picture window over the bathtub (deep, wide, with molded armrests and Jacuzzi jets) looked out over the sky and the ocean. I took deep breaths, squinted and tried to imagine the bathroom a pearly white, then I closed my eyes and tried to image it Caribbean Blue. So much seemed to depend on the color I picked—the person I would be in that room, the marriage I would have, the life I would lead—but I couldn't imagine a color that would make it all work.

I got out my phone and called Vanessa.

"Do you have a few minutes?"

"Is something wrong?" she asked.

"No, I just can't pick a color of paint."

"I'm on my way," she said. "But is something wrong?"

"No, everything's fine. It's great."

"And when I show up you're going to tell me, what? That someone's died, someone has some incurable disease?"

"I had a mammogram yesterday."

"I knew it."

"It was fine," I said.

"But if it wasn't fine, you weren't going to tell me, were you? You were going to wait until we picked out a paint color for the wall or maybe until after we'd had lunch and a stroll on the beach. You're so bad that way."

"But it *was* fine."

"And you're lucky, too, because you would've pissed me off if something were wrong."

"So can you come?"

"I'll be there in five minutes," she said.

While I waited for Vanessa to cross the street and walk up the stairs, I looked again at the colors. Light beige or dark beige? Sky blue or cerulean blue? How could this decision be so difficult?

Vanessa walked in, walked right over, and grabbed me. She wasn't tall or particularly strong, but she had a fierce hug. She pressed herself into you and gave you the feeling that she wouldn't let go.

"It was five years ago this week," I said.

"It was a Monday," Vanessa said, "and this is a Wednesday, and five years is an amazing milestone so we should have a party."

"You know how I feel about parties."

"There should be margaritas. And a band. Wouldn't it be fun to have a band?"

"We're moving in less than a week. Christmas is in a week and I'm on deadline for a piece on organic cotton lingerie. We're not having a party."

"OK, then we'll go out to dinner somewhere fabulous. Maybe Rick can get us into the dining room out at the golf course since he's building half their houses. They have the most fantastic sushi salad."

"Rick and I haven't had sex in three months," I blurted. We hadn't, in fact, had sex in more than six months, but six months sounded far worse than three and I wasn't ready to admit it, even to my best friend.

Vanessa laughed. She was certain three months without sex was an exaggeration.

"I'm not joking," I said. "We probably couldn't even agree on how to do it. We can't agree on anything. I do five hours of legwork finding tumbled marble tile to match the granite and Rick takes one look and says, 'It looks washed-out to me.' Last week, I gave him printouts of the Whirlpool washer and dryer I wanted, and he didn't even look at them before telling me that he's putting Maytags in his golf course houses, as if everyone knows that Maytags are better than Whirlpools. And don't even get me started about the food thing. We're spending four hundred thousand dollars on this remodel and he won't spend forty dollars on dinner out."

"I bet he likes the beige," Vanessa said, pointing to a swatch on the wall that was just barely off white.

"It's called Swiss Coffee," I said. "It's the color he's painted every house he's ever built. I think he gets a kick-back on it from Benjamin Moore—you know, paint three houses, get the fourth one free."

"But that turquoise is the best."

"It's called Caribbean Blue."

"It's perfect."

"I had to beg him to put up the swatch. He says it'll take three coats of Swiss Coffee just to cover it up."

"So we're just rubber stamping Rick's beige?" Vanessa asked.

"Basically."

"You should have married a lawyer."

"Or a banker. I bet the wives of bankers get to pick the color they want on their bathroom walls."

Vanessa looked at her watch. "I'm showing a house in Rolling Hills," she said, then put her hand on my shoulder. "The beige will be fine."

"Thanks for coming."

"Hey," she said, as she turned to go down the stairs, "as long as you're out researching lingerie, maybe you should pick up something sexy for yourself. It sounds like you could use it." She disappeared down the steps.

"And about the party," she yelled from downstairs, "don't think you're getting away without one."

Organic lingerie in any fabric used to be a rather scratchy affair. You could buy underwear made from wool or linen, and some very rough stuff made from hemp, but the aesthetic was definitely utilitarian. All that changed after Patagonia and Nike started using organic fiber in their sportswear lines. The price came down low enough for fashion designers to go green, and now there was something of a revolution going on. The other day I interviewed the owner of a company in Ohio that made a line of bras and bikini underwear from pure organic cotton. They were dyed bright, happy colors and cut in modern shapes like boy shorts and thongs. She couldn't keep them in stock. Today, I was talking to the proprietor of Avisha, an upscale lingerie shop in Redondo Village. She carried a line of lingerie called Good Karma, made entirely of organic cotton, and I wanted to run the fabric between my fingers so I could say something coherent about how it felt against the skin.

"Bonjour," Manon said. "You must be April."

"It's nice to meet you," I said, and shook her hand. "Thanks for making time for me."

"Come this way," she said. She led me to a dressing area, where she had laid out a selection of Good Karma items on a padded bench. "These have a very nice shape and beautiful trim," she said. "Do you see?" She handed me a chemise with an inset of lace just under the bust. It was a natural white with a tropical floral pattern. The cotton was very soft and had an earthy heft.

"This designer understands her fabric," Manon explained. "She has used it to her advantage. She is more like a French woman than an American that way."

I know a woman who just came back from a three-year stint as an expat in Paris. The thing she missed the most, she said, was the lingerie. Women in France spent far more money on their lingerie than their American counterparts. If they had a windfall of $500, they'd splurge on a made-to-measure bra from a shop on the Rue des Saints-Pères, whose proprietor, everyone knew, was the granddaughter of a woman who had been a corsetiere to queens. These women could have conversations about the difference between cheap Chinese silk and the finer quality French or Italian. Cotton was not discussed. "I understand that the French lingerie designers aren't using much organic cotton," I said.

"The French are very attached to their stretch lace," confirmed Manon.

I scribbled her words in my notebook. "So you don't feel that the organic fabrics will gain worldwide appeal?"

"In lingerie? No," she said. She walked across the shop and took down a bra and a matching pair of panties that looked like a confection spun of sugar. The bra was a deep chocolate brown, with turquoise blue accents.

The cups were brown lace with turquoise appliqués. The straps were delicately rolled—two small strings on each side. Beneath the cups and around the back was a band of stretchy swirled lace, which was echoed in the waistband of the panties. "You simply can't make a brassiere like this without nylon and spandex," Manon said, "and nothing in the world fits like this or feels like this." She then held out the set to me. "Try," she said. "You'll see."

I shook my head. "I had a mastectomy," I said, as if these four words were enough to explain why I wasn't a candidate for expensive lingerie.

"Come try it," she said, placing the bra in a dressing room. "You will be surprised."

I stood there, mute, unmoving.

"Come." She held her hand out to the dressing room, and because it seemed rude to say no to someone who had agreed to help me, I followed her. She shut the door. I peeled off my sweater, unhooked my gray, pilling bra and slipped into the chocolate lace. Over my plain beige, high-hipped underwear, I pulled the brown and turquoise lace panties.

"How is it?" Manon asked. She was standing right outside the dressing room, waiting for me to appear. I had a jagged hip to hip scar where they had harvested the skin and fat needed to rebuild my breast. I had scars around my belly button, which was not a belly button at all, but a twist of flesh manufactured after the real belly button had been taken away. There was a circular scar running around my fake breast, tiny scars where they had created the nipple in the same way as the belly button, and a long scar running from the breast up under my armpit. The bra was light as air, yet somehow substantial. The size discrepancy between my breasts seemed as if it had been erased.

I opened the door.

Manon beamed and clapped her hands. "Beautiful, no? Just wait a moment," she said. "Let me get you something to try so you can see how this changes the lines of your body. Your husband will love it." She was back in a moment with a brown silk knit dress. It was a pullover with a shirred waistline and a deep V neckline.

I laughed. "That would look great on my daughter,"

I said. Jackie was two inches taller than me and eighty pounds lighter. Her hair shimmered, her hips swayed, her skin was flawless. She looked fantastic in everything and I simply looked like somebody's mother.

"Nonsense," Manon said. "Come. Try it."

I closed the door again and shimmied into the dress. It was so tight I had to yank it down over my rear end, but once I had it on, I turned to the side. The snug fit over the perfect bra made my body look voluptuous instead of lumpy. The drape of the wraparound made my waist look trim. I made a sound that must have seemed like approval.

"You see!" Manon exclaimed when I opened the door. "Gorgeous! Organic cotton is a good idea for relaxing. Good for the planet. But it cannot do this for a woman."

I changed back into my own sad bra, put on my clothes and stepped out of the dressing room. On the coffee table next to the padded bench where the organic cotton had been displayed was the new issue of *Town & Country*. I was holding my notepad in my hands. "You mentioned that my husband would love the outfit you selected," I said, casually, as if I were still digging for facts for my story. "Do you have a lot of men buying lingerie for their wives during the holidays?"

Manon laughed. "Oh, yes," she said.

"I take it they don't go for the organic cotton?"

"Perhaps," she said, "if they are buying something to be a comfort. It is so soft, you know. But men like for their wives to be shapely and sexy." She held up the bra and panties I'd just taken off. "They usually select something like this."

I thanked Manon, then drove away from Avisha down to the Esplanade and sat there looking at the winter beach. The waves broke steeply down from their crests and crashed hard on the sand. The water was in a muddy froth as it spilled onto the beach. There were two bulldozers a few blocks away pushing sand into huge mounds to preserve it for the summer. When Jackie was little, we'd climb up the steep sides of the dunes—two steps up, one step back—then race down the far face. We'd pick a tire track and follow it half a mile down the beach, trying to keep our footprints within the outlines and analyzing her little steps compared to my big ones. I'd forgotten to come to the beach the whole time we'd been working on the house. How could I have forgotten how pretty it was in the winter? And how could I have left that lingerie store without even seeing the price tag on the chocolate brown bra?

I looked at my watch and pulled away from the curb. I took the first left away from the crashing quiet of the beach and sped down the block, but when I got to the stop sign at the end, I turned around and went back. That block was one of a dozen seaside lanes that ran perpendicular to the Esplanade. During the early part of the century, when Redondo Beach boasted a resort hotel, where Hollywood stars and well-to-do-families splashed in the big indoor pool and danced in the high-ceilinged hall, a cluster of bungalows sprung up on these streets. They were built by hand in the California Craftsman tradition—casual houses for weekends by the sea. They were within steps of the steep stairs that led down to the sand and came with the promise of a screen door slamming in the breeze as sunburned kids scurried down to the beach. On the street I had chosen to speed down that afternoon, there was only one beach bungalow left. It stood in the middle of the block on the south side of the street surrounded by Mediterranean mansions, modern glass boxes and Spanish-style villas.

It was for sale.

I parked the car at the curb and rolled down my window for a better view. Even though the houses surrounding it were all far grander and more modern—houses that had been remodeled just like mine to accommodate families who had a pressing need for travertine-tiled entryways, high-capacity washers and dryers, and walk-in closets big enough for a bed—the bungalow felt like the most important house on the street. It had a presence to it. It sat on its piece of ground as if it had sprung up organically. I had spent so much time over the last year looking at slick photos of big houses and scouting out materials and appliances in huge showrooms, that I had forgotten what an authentic home even looked like.

The house sat on a small patch of lawn behind a white picket fence. It was wrapped in white clapboard, and each of its windows was outlined in hunter green trim as if drawn in by a child. The front porch was like an invitation. It extended from one side to the other—a long, wide expanse large enough to hold a porch swing, a bench, a table and two chairs and six pots of lavender, with their chaos of long purple stems. A gently arched beam framed the opening of the porch, held up by square tapered columns. Two tall windows flanked the large front door—each with an etched transom above it that looked as though it came from a completely different time and place. In the center of the front door was an enormous pine bough wreath tied with a red bow.

The yard was lush and overrun. Along the front of the house was a riot of winter flowers: lavender, salvia and tiny white-dotted rosemary. Running down the side yard nearest to me was a cement driveway with a strip of grass in the middle, and at the end of the drive was a garage with big, wide doors whose windows matched the ones on the front door. Eucalyptus trees towered above the house from the backyard, and there were palm, lemon and lime trees along the drive.

The thing I thought about as I sat in my car, transfixed by that house, was a piece of art I'd seen seventeen years before. I'd gone to a conference on early childhood education in Portland, Oregon. During one of the afternoons off, I went to lunch with a group of new teachers at a restaurant across from an art gallery. We sat outside eating our sandwiches and I kept looking at that gallery as if someone were looking back. Hanging in the window were enormous black-and-white canvases depicting trees—an oak tree, a pine tree, one of those cypress trees that jut out over the water in Monterey. They were just black branches on a white background, sparse and eerie. After dessert, I went across the street to take a closer look. It turned out the trees were drawn with ballpoint pen on paper. The artist had made a hundred thousand tiny strokes, creating shape and shade with nothing more than little black marks. I stepped into the gallery to gawk and hungrily sought out the price tag of the pine tree, my favorite. It was $10,000.

I can remember so clearly the feeling I had standing in that gallery looking at those trees. I wanted one. I wanted to take one home with me and put it on my wall, but $10,000 was almost half my salary. All I could do was stand and stare.

～

"She's crazy," someone said, from somewhere just out-side my car. I flinched and looked out the window to see a white-haired woman in a pink sweat suit walking two small white poodles.

"Excuse me?" I said. I wasn't sure she had spoken to me, but there was no one else on the sidewalk.

"Mrs. Torrey. The owner. She has some harebrained idea to sell that house to someone who won't tear it down. Of course everyone else on this block has already torn their old bungalow down and made a fortune in the process. Peg Torrey doesn't care about any of that. After Harry died—he was her husband—I'm afraid she's gone 'round the bend."

I smiled. I had no idea what to say, and the poodle lady took my silence as an invitation to carry on.

"The daughter just wants Peg out of the house before she hurts herself," she said. "And all of us"—she swept her free hand across the street, taking in every house on the block—"would just like to see someone move in here who'll keep the lawn mowed."

I smiled again, feeling like a prisoner in my own car.

"I'd put in a good word for you, if I thought it'd matter," she continued, "but Peg Torrey doesn't think much of me, I'm afraid, after that business with the fence in '97."

I sensed my opening. "Well, thank you," I said, quickly, and turned the key in the ignition.

When I pulled away, the neighbor was standing on the curb waving to me as if I were heading out on a long journey.

~

I'd only left myself an hour and a half to write a draft of the lingerie piece. I quoted a woman from the Organic Trade Association about how traditionally grown cotton is the most polluting crop on the planet, and then talked about the sportswear companies' lead in creating a market for organic farming that had now trickled down to the lingerie niche. I talked about doing good, feeling good and looking good, and then headed over to the high school to watch Jackie's volleyball game.

I climbed onto the bleachers in the gym and took my place next to Gina, one of the other moms, whose daughter was the star setter for the team and who was expected to receive a scholarship to UCLA when recruiting decisions were announced next fall. I'd sat through hundreds of hours of volleyball with this mom. Our role was to sit and watch, and to know when a back row attack was illegal or when the players were running a five-one offense. The girls rarely looked our way. After the games, they headed for the locker rooms, and the cars of the kids who had their drivers' licenses, and you'd think that they didn't even know we were there, or care that we were there, but they did. Once, the coach yelled at Jackie for being in the wrong place on the final point of a tie-breaker. He towered over her—a large man with a loud voice, pointing his finger and barking at her for making a mistake in a ball game—and as I watched her eyes tear up and her shoulders slump, I decided I couldn't stand the silent witnessing any longer.

"What did he say to you?" I asked when we got in the car. I was picking a fight and she knew it.

"Who?" she asked.

"Coach Ben."

"When?"

I took a deep breath. "When he benched you after the tie-breaker."

"That I'd been playing too long to make a stupid mistake like that."

"He can't talk to you that way," I insisted.

"He talks to everyone that way, Mom," she said. "You can't take it personally."

"You're saying it doesn't bother you?"

"Of course it bothers me."

"Then why put up with it?"

"It's part of the game."

"It shouldn't be."

"Well, it is."

"Then it's a part I don't choose to watch."

"Meaning what?"

"Meaning that if I have to sit there and watch him yell at you like that, I don't know if I'm going to come anymore. I can't stand it."

"Do whatever you want," she said.

But later that night when I went into her room to say good night to her, Jackie stopped me in the dark.

"Mom?" she asked, in the voice of a little girl. "I like it when you come to my games."

And so I was there.

Midway through the first game, Gina nudged my side. "Who's the boy?" she asked.

I scanned the gym and immediately saw who she was talking about. A tall boy with shoulder-length bleached-out blond hair was sitting alone on the bleachers near the net. He was following Jackie's every movement with a look on his face somewhere between rapture and the way you look when you have the flu. If I thought my daughter was lovely, this boy was closer to something you would call glorious, if only because of the way he seemed to glow as he watched her. If I had been a photographer, I would have made a fortune capturing his profile for a Gap ad, or an Abercrombie billboard. If I had been a builder of boy bands, I would have tapped this one to be my lead singer, whether he could carry a tune or not.

"I have no idea," I said. I couldn't take my eyes off the boy who couldn't take his eyes off Jackie. I felt an odd affinity for him. My relationship with my daughter was mostly about my watching her. I sat on the sidelines at volleyball games, sat in the driver's seat as we drove to the orthodontist or a tournament somewhere down in Orange Country. I sat on the periphery as she took tests and went to dances and went to the movies with her friends. Occasionally, I offered a suggestion about something—which colleges to put on the list of possibilities or which dress looked better of two she was considering—but mostly I just watched. I was like this boy: sitting on the sidelines, taking it all in, unable to turn away.

"He looks like he's in love," Gina said.

"Can you be in love at age fifteen?" I asked.

"Romeo and Juliet were only fourteen," she said. "Love at first sight knows no age limits."

Rick and I weren't kids when we met—I was twenty-six, he was twenty-nine—and it didn't take us long to realize what we felt for each other. After our third date, he took me to his parents' house for dinner. I was fretting about what to wear and what to take as a hostess gift, when Rick just stopped, took me by the shoulders and said, "April. Listen to me. My mother will be making brownies from a box for dessert. She has pet ducks. It's going to be fine."

It was more than fine. Julia Newton's house was framed by beds of iceberg rose bushes, which she tended herself. There was a little gurgling brook with a pond for the ducks, who would parade around after her. She did, indeed, have a thing for brownies from a box and always had a row of Betty Crocker in her pantry. Her couches were all comfortable; her rooms were all large and airy. She had done the books for the family plumbing business when it operated out of one small warehouse and later ran the whole accounting department. I liked her from the moment I laid eyes on her, and I was desperate that she like me.

I needn't have worried. When it came time for dessert, she asked me to help her in the kitchen. The brownies had twenty minutes left to cook, but she pulled them out of the oven, took a tub of whipped cream cheese out of the refrigerator and said to me, "This is the secret family recipe."

"Cream cheese?"

She nodded. "You swirl it through with twenty minutes left to go and the boxed brownies become instantly gourmet."

"Sounds good," I said.

"I thought you should know."

I had been dating her son for three weeks; I had met her less than three hours before. I was having trouble following what she was saying.

"You and Rick are a very good match," she said, and then I got it—and not only that, I agreed. I was in love, maybe not at first sight, but it was love with a good man who loved me back. I blushed.

I turned from my trance back to the volleyball game just in time to see the tangle of arms and the ball come down on Jackie's outstretched hand, and Jackie fall to the ground and scream. I got to her at the same time as the blond boy and the coach. The boy put his hand on her bare sweaty shoulder. I'd like to say that I was focused on my child's finger and the way it was bent and the wincing of her face, but mostly what I saw was that boy's hand on her bare sweaty shoulder. His skin was darker than hers by several shades, and his hand was large and lean. He was gripping her so hard that I could see the white indentations underneath each finger pad.

I had done exactly the same thing when, at the age of eight or ten, Jackie would throw a fit over having to brush her teeth or pick up her pajamas off the bedroom floor. She was too old for fits, but not yet old enough to know how to stop them, and her body was not yet so removed from mine that I couldn't help. I would take each of her shoulders in one of my hands and squeeze, and as calmly as I could manage, I would say, "Jackie, stop." It was usually more like a scream. It was me screaming at her to get her to stop screaming. I may not have mastered the voice, but the hands worked. And now this boy, whose name I didn't even know, had his hands in the exact same place where I had so often placed mine.

"It's broken," her coach said, turning his head my

way. It took me a moment to realize that he was talking to me, that he was instructing me.

"OK," I said, and watched as the boy helped Jackie to her feet, his hand grasping hers, his hand under her elbow, her body leaning into his. "I'll run and get the car."

He was sitting with her on a low wall when I pulled up next to the gym. She had an ice pack in her hand. The long strands of hair that had escaped her ponytail were wet and straggly. Her shorts were extremely short. He leapt up, opened the door and leaned down, his blond hair falling in front of his eyes.

"I'll call," he said.

She nodded. She probably smiled, but I couldn't see her face.

In the moment before he slammed the door, I almost asked if he'd like to come, but I knew he would say yes.

"You OK?" I asked, as we pulled away.

She leaned her head against the headrest and closed her eyes. When we hit the long stoplight at the corner of Anza and Sepulveda, she sucked at her teeth and made a kind of moan, but she didn't cry and she didn't offer any information about the boy.

The emergency room was jammed. There were people sitting on every available chair and people sitting on the floor. There were women holding babies and whole families sitting together in grim rows. The strange thing was that no one looked like they were in trauma. We stood in line to speak to the intake nurse, and overheard the conversations: someone had a sore throat, another person had an ear infection. After we filled out the paperwork and called Rick, I found Jackie a place to sit in an orange plastic chair next to a tinsel Christmas tree and pushed her hair behind her ears the way I always did when she was throwing up.

"Is that enough ice?" I asked.

She nodded.

"You're not going to pass out, are you?"

She shook her head.

I put my hand on the back of her neck as if I could hold it in place. "Do you want me to call Mrs. Hennessy to see if you won?" I asked.

"Max said he'd call," she said.

"The blond?"

She nodded.

Twenty minutes after we arrived, Rick sped in. He knelt in front of Jackie and kissed her forehead, where the sweat had dried and plastered her hair to her skin. "It hurts like hell, doesn't it?"

She smiled a little and nodded. "I had the spike, too," she said. "That idiot Michelle stepped in front of me. It was clearly my ball."

Rick kissed her again, then turned to me. "How long do they say it'll be?"

"Forty-five minutes until she's called to the back room, but from the look of this crowd, I'd say it'll be double that time."

"I can't wait that long," Jackie whined. "I can't. It hurts."

Rick jumped up and marched to the receptionist's desk.

"Oh, great," Jackie said, "now he's going to make unreasonable demands of the underpaid staff." She dropped her head into her good hand, causing her ponytail to flop over and swing near the orange carpet.

"How do you know they're underpaid?"

"A.P. Spanish," she said, without lifting her head. "We had this woman come in and talk to us about immigration and the jobs the people from Mexico get in this country and how we exploit them so we don't have to do any of our own dirty work."

I glanced at Rick, standing near the woman behind the desk. "That woman is African American," I said.

Jackie shrugged. "America is an equal opportunity exploiter."

"It looks like Dad's got her attention."

She flipped her hair back in place and slumped back in the chair. "He does that at hospitals," she said. "He makes a big fuss, and also he prays. You can't tell about the prayer unless you know he's doing it. He just sits there and closes his eyes and kind of moves his mouth like a fish. It's pretty embarrassing unless you're Muslim. I mean, Muslims are supposed to pray in public. Five times a day this bell rings and they drop everything they're doing and everyone prays."

"Did you learn this in A.P. Spanish, too?"

"History, Mom," she said. She paused a moment, as

if measuring the breadth and depth of my ignorance. "Do you believe that God really sent his son to earth as a poor fatherless carpenter three thousand years ago?" she asked.

I was about to make a quip about the influence of *The DaVinci Code* on an entire generation of religious thought, but I stopped myself. Her questions had that ring of importance that moments with your kids can sometimes have, when you know it will matter more than the others. I'd been trying for years to understand the phenomenon so that I could write about it in a cover story for *Parents* or *Parenting,* or more likely *Child*, but I could never wrap my hands around it enough to make a convincing pitch. "No," I said, "I don't believe that."

"Have you ever believed it?"

"I pretended to one summer at church camp when they asked everyone who considered Jesus their Lord and Savior to raise their hands one night during the campfire program. Jefferey Dobbs raised his hand next to me, so I raised mine, too."

"It's hard to believe it really happened."

"But it's such a nice story," I said. "I love the innkeeper. I played Mary one year when we lived in Pennsylvania, and I got to wear the light blue satin headpiece, but I secretly wished I'd been the innkeeper."

"So you like the story and that's why you believe in God and that's why we've gone to church all these years?"

"No," I said. "I like the story and I also believe in God. But I'm not sure the story is true, and we've gone to church all these years mostly out of habit."

"That's pretty lame, Mom."

I was about to say that I knew it was lame. I had, in fact, recently been struggling mightily with the fact that it was lame, but before I could make my confession, Jackie's cell phone rang. I dug it out of her purse and handed it to her.

"Sweet!" she said. Then, "Are you serious?" There was a moment of silence, then she said, "Both my parents, actually." She listened again, then said, "That's so sweet." And finally, "I'll call you as soon as I get home."

Ten minutes later, Jackie was called to an interior

waiting room, and fifteen minutes after that, she went into the X-ray room. Rick stepped into the hallway to make a phone call. I picked up a battered copy of *Woman's Day* and read about recipes for slow cooker suppers, then leafed through an old *Car and Driver*. A very large woman with a very large soda cup in her hand set down a copy of the *Beach Reporter*, our free local newspaper. I sometimes read it when I walk on the treadmill at the gym, mesmerized by poorly written stories about aging surf legends and health spa openings.

"May I look at that?" I asked.

"'S not mine," she said. "You can do whatever you want."

"Thanks," I said.

I scanned the headlines—a local boy had been killed in Fallujah; a sophomore from Hermosa Beach was the backup kicker for USC's Rose Bowl team—then I flipped inside. Someone had taken out a whole-page ad on page two. A moment after I registered the oddity of such a big ad in the *Beach Reporter*, I registered what it was: a photo of the house I had seen on Pepper Tree Lane. The elegant headline spread across the whole page:

FOR SALE: THE LAST BEACH BUNGALOW

The owner of this 1928 original bungalow is seeking a buyer with heart. What would you give—besides money— to live here? Bring your offers, your stories and a promise to preserve and protect. Winner will pay $300,000.

Open House, Saturday 1 to 4

My heart began to pound.

I glanced at the fat lady with the Coke, who had her nose buried in a *People* with George Clooney on the cover, then I ripped the page from the newspaper, folded it and tucked it into my purse, where I now had a little library of stolen print. The fat lady didn't even flinch, but my pulse was racing.

Seconds later, Rick walked in.

"You OK?" he asked.

I shrugged, mostly to keep from squirming. I had that uncomfortable feeling I was about to be caught.

"I've broken three or four fingers," he said. "She'll be fine."

The articles in my purse seemed like they were on fire. I could feel their heat and their danger, pressing through the leather that sat near my feet. "It's not that," I blurted, and the second I said it, I knew there was no going back. "It's the house, actually. The whole thing is starting to make me kind of sick."

"People always feel like that toward the end of a project," Rick said. "It's like buyer's remorse, only ten times worse, because you've bought all these parts hoping they'll add up to a whole and you've never built a house before so you're not sure they're all going to fall into place. But it will work. Believe me."

"It's no wonder your clients love you," I said. "You're smooth as silk."

Rick smiled and took my hand. He was, in fact, something of a genius when it came to designing and building houses for our particular microclimate. He used copious amounts of glass, designing whole walls that could swing open to let in the light, but those same walls shut tight as a drum against the sea breeze and the fog. He liked sandblasted wood that tied the interior to the textures and colors of the beach and granite in warm red and orange tones.

He presented me with the design for our new house on the first day of the new millennium, which was just three weeks after my mastectomy. I was still bandaged and sore, still fragile and sad. I was afraid to get off the couch. He came out of his office on that day and called Jackie out to sit with us. She was only ten. He was holding a roll of paper tied with a red bow.

"What's this?" I asked.

"Do you remember what you said to me the night you were diagnosed?"

I could, in fact, remember everything I said with excruciating detail. That day was like a shiny coin that I could pull out of my pocket and twirl in my fingers. There, etched into one side, were the exact expressions on people's faces, the precise tone of the doctor's declaration, the words I uttered to Rick when I called, hysterical, to tell him the astounding news. On the other side was the way I begged Rick to call my mother because I couldn't bear to hear her shock or receive her sympathy, the way it appeared as if everyone walking down the street was suddenly so fragile, and Jackie's endless questions—where did the cancer come from; how will the doctors get it out; will I get it, too; are you going to die?—and the way I patiently answered each one as if I knew what I was talking about.

"I said a lot of things that night," I said.

Jackie piped in: "She said you should find a new wife and that I shouldn't be afraid to let someone else be my mom."

Rick squeezed Jackie's hand and smiled at her—a smile full of obvious sorrow that a ten-year-old would have a memory like that in her head—then turned back toward me. "You said that it would be a shame to have to die in such a shabby house."

I nodded. "I do remember saying that."

"You said that we'd waited too long to build our dream house."

"Well, yeah," I said, "because we had such big plans when we moved in here."

"And I've spent far too much time building other

people's dream houses," he said. "Now it's our turn." He handed me the paper.

I slipped off the bow, knowing exactly what I would find inside. Blue lines crisscrossing blue paper, outlining a big, open kitchen, an office with built-in everything and a huge master bath oriented perfectly to capture the morning sun. Glass would be called out for the entire wall facing the ocean and sandblasted beams for the entryway. There would be bamboo floors, granite counters, tumbled marble tile in a kitchen with hand-rubbed oversized cabinets. He had done all this work while I was in the hospital, while I was waiting for toxic chemicals to drip into my veins, while I was throwing up, while I was asleep.

"Are you serious?" I asked quietly.

Rick nodded. He leaned down, buried his face in my neck and held on to the arm on my good side. "I love you so much," he said. When he lifted his face it was wet, and the look on Jackie's face was one of absolute terror. Her dad hadn't said one word about building a house before it was too late. He hadn't said one single thing about building a house as a fortress against an uncertain future. But her dad had cried. He didn't have to speak.

When I was done with chemo, many months later, Rick submitted the plans to the city. We lived in an area that requires you to flag all additions and remodels for six months to give the neighbors time to complain if you're blocking their views. We sailed through that trial, but turned up an engineering problem on the back property line and had to build a retaining wall before we could proceed with the house itself. Grief delayed us next. Rick's parents were sideswiped by a semitruck on their way home from a Dodger game. Their car flipped, it rolled, and they were dead by the time the paramedics came.

It was one of those accidents you hear about on rush-hour radio with numbing regularity, but you never think that someone's parents died; you always just think of how jammed the freeway's going to be. Rick's older brother, Dennis, got the call from the California Highway Patrol, but Dennis lived five hundred miles away. It was Rick who went to identify the bodies, and Rick who sat down with the minister to pick the hymns and prayers for the memorial service and Rick who ushered his parents' wills through a year of probate. By the time we were whole enough again to think about working on the house, it was nearly four years from the day when Rick gave me the plans. And now here it was, a week until we moved back in, just a week before the Christmas of Jackie's junior year in high school, the week I was five-years free of cancer, and we were sitting in a hospital waiting room just like we had before.

"Thank you," Rick said, dismissing my praise about his smoothness with clients and my fears about the house. "And don't worry. You're going to adore this house." He kissed my hand, and then leaned over to pick up *Car and Driver* off the waiting room coffee table.

A minute later, I said, "I think Jackie has a boyfriend," but Rick didn't hear me. He was so engrossed in a three-year-old article about Toyota's plans for world domination that I could have started belting out the National Anthem and he wouldn't have heard me. "I think they're pretty serious," I continued, "or at least physical. I think that's it. I think they're physical." I caught a movement out of the corner of my eye. When I glanced over, I saw the fat lady staring at me.

"You talkin' to me?" she demanded.

"No." I shrugged, waving my arm in the air toward Rick. "My husband."

"Good," she said. " 'Cause I don't want to be knowin' nothin' about nobody's boyfriend."

RIDAY

In the early years of parenting, you'll give anything for twenty minutes free and clear of your kids. You pray for nighttime, when the noise will stop, the hunger will stop, the accidents will stop, the incessant questions about the moon, the sky, the ocean, the cat next door, the cow on TV, the telephone and toy in the bottom of the cereal box—will stop. But in the teen years, you'll give anything for twenty minutes in the same room with your kids. You'll pay a ransom for a conversation, a bribe for just a little time. I imagined that Jackie would stay home to nurse her broken finger, which meant I could have a whole day with her. My work could wait. We'd go get smoothies, do some Christmas shopping. I still didn't know what to get her. There was nothing she didn't have, nothing she seemed to need. A few hours walking through the shops in Redondo Village might give me a clue.

When she was little, I used to love Christmas. I saved every single one of the letters she carefully wrote out to Santa, about wanting a real wooden train with a tunnel, or the red patent leather shoes for her American Girl doll, because they were requests I could so easily meet. For just a few hundred dollars, I could make her world complete. After church on Christmas Eve, Rick and I would stay up late wrapping all the presents we'd amassed and constructing some tangible proof that Santa had actually come to our house. We scattered ashes from the fireplace, kicked oatmeal around the front yard as if the reindeers had gotten their snouts into the food we'd laid out. We'd eat the sugar cookies, drink the milk, fill the stockings and wait to be awakened by Jackie's squeals of delight.

Christmas began to change when Jackie turned six. That was the year she decided she wanted a dog. It was no longer enough to talk to all the dogs we passed when we rode bikes through our neighborhood, or to play with the dogs whose owners snuck them down to the beach to play in the surf. It was no longer enough that other people's dogs would immediately come to her and lick her hand or bring her a ball to toss. She wanted a dog of her own—one who would sleep at the foot of her bed and wait for her when she came home from school and sit with her while she read. She asked Santa for a dog, but this was one thing I couldn't deliver.

I can't stand dogs. I can't stand the way they jump all over you and lick you and never swerve from their high-demand status. I hate the way people treat their dogs like children, with hand-fixed meals and veterinarians who make house calls. I once read a Billy Collins poem about a dog—how the dog trots out the door every morning with only a brown coat and blue collar and how this is such a fine example of a life without encumbrance and how the dog would be a paragon of earthly detachment if it weren't for the fact that the poet is the dog's god.

That was the last line: "If only I were not her god." I remember thinking, *That's it. That's exactly it.* I couldn't get Jackie a dog for Christmas because I would have to be the dog's god, and that was something I couldn't be.

So Santa brought soft stuffed Huskies and pug-nosed mutts, a whole veterinarian set with fifteen kinds of plastic dogs, and one year, a life-sized Saint Bernard posed in a sitting position with his tongue hanging out, but it was never enough. Jackie began to get angry at Santa. She began to wonder why he didn't listen, why he was so mean, why he brought Julia Bertucci a King Charles Cavalier cocker spaniel puppy on Christmas morning when he only brought Jackie a calendar that featured a picture of the same thing.

What, after a certain point, can you say? You tell the truth and then Christmas becomes something else entirely.

~

"How are you feeling?" I asked, when Jackie came out of her room the morning after the incident with the broken finger. It was 7:00 A.M. and she was dressed for school: jeans, flip-flops, two layered T-shirts, eyeliner, lipgloss.

"Fine," she said, giving me a wiggly-fingered wave.

"You're OK to go to school?"

She shrugged her shoulders—*why not?*—then said, "We're finishing our card sale today," as if this fact made it obvious why she had to go. The cards were part of her midterm project in history. She and three other girls had been conducting a lunchtime fund-raiser. For three dollars, students and teachers could purchase a holiday card, an envelope, postage and the address of a soldier in Iraq. There was a big bucket of pens at the table, and right there, without having to even think about it, they could send a holiday greeting to a soldier overseas. With the money they made from the cards, the girls were going to buy chocolate bars to send with each box of greetings. So far, they'd collected 250 pieces of mail.

"I can come pick you up before practice," I said.

"I'm staying for practice."

"Jackie, don't be ridiculous."

"I can run, I can do sit-ups. The doctor said that if it

doesn't hurt in a week, I can hit, so I'll probably be able to play the Holiday Classic."

I closed my eyes and took a deep breath. It's hard to argue with a child who is a patriotic, vegetarian, straight-A student who exercises every day and cares about the working poor. It's hard to argue when you feel as if your child has her life more together than you do. "Fine," I said, "but promise me you'll call if it starts to hurt."

"I promise," she said, in a sing-song voice. She gave me a quick hug and then waltzed out the door.

~

After Jackie left, I pulled the stack of pilfered papers out of my purse. I slipped the *Town & Country* piece into a folder marked "Ideas" and spread the newspaper ad out on my desk. Who would sell a house like that in a contest? And what did it mean, *Bring your stories?* I did a Google search on "house contests, Los Angeles, beach cities," and came up with a list of organizations that had raffled off million-dollar homes as fund-raising stunts. For the price of a raffle ticket—$150—you could gain the chance to win a home in Palos Verdes, Santa Barbara or Malibu. Farther down the Google list, there was a series of entries about a contest for a Manhattan Beach house that had ended in a lawsuit when it was revealed that the winner was the husband of the owner's niece. On page three, there was an entry about a guy in Venice Beach who was going to raze a nine-hundred-square-foot bungalow built in 1906 and was offering it free to anyone who would move it, serious inquiries only.

I remembered driving North to the Boundary Waters one summer when I was a kid, living in Minnesota. We had a station wagon that year, and I liked to count the other station wagons we passed along the way. As I watched from the backseat we rolled by a flatbed truck whose cargo was half a house. The house had been sliced completely in half, like a cake, and I could see inside the walls and the floor, under the skin of that house. I held my breath until we were completely past, and then I turned around and craned my neck to watch it behind us.

"Did you see that?" I asked. "There was a house on a truck. They cut it in half."

"You're such a doofus," my brother said, shoving me in the stomach with his elbow. He was blessed with the ability to read in the car and had his head buried in a comic book.

"They unbolt it from the foundation," my dad explained, "and lift it right off for transportation." He was a manager at a company that manufactured furniture. The year before that, he had been a manager at a company that made china plates and cups. In a few years, he would be a manager for something else and we would be moving again, leaving our house and whatever friends I'd managed to make when I finally figured out what kind of jeans the kids wore to school in that town.

"You can take your house with you when you move?" I asked. My heart was pounding in my chest, my throat, my ears. We had left a house with an attic playroom and another with a three-car garage. My room in the house in Minnesota had two small windows that looked out over a steeply pitched roof. The windows were like two eyes that looked out onto the world. I loved to sit at those windows and read late into the night—stories about other girls in other houses in other places in other times. There were little houses on prairies and big houses in cities, houses with servants and houses with curtains that could be made into dresses. Sometimes I drew sketches of the houses so that I could get a better idea how far away the kitchen was from the dining room, or where, exactly, a big hallway led. Moving to the next place where Dad had a job—a better job! more responsibility!—wouldn't be half as bad if I could take that room with me.

"I suppose you *could* take a house with you," my mother chimed in, "though it's just wallboard and wood. I don't know why anyone would want to."

I was around thirteen years old, and it was the first instance where I knew without a shadow of a doubt that my mother was wrong. The possibility of her flawed nature had occurred to me before that moment, of course—sometimes around the topic of blue jeans and hairstyles, but most often around the topic of my dad. He watched a lot of hockey. He took frequent business trips that seemed to center around his secretary.

No matter what job he took, there invariably materialized an unfair boss, a boss who was a jerk, a boss my
dad couldn't tolerate. I wouldn't understand until I was
much older that my dad was a philandering flake, but
at thirteen, I understood that my mom was putting up
with a lot for what she seemed to be getting out of her
marriage. The moment she said that a house was nothing more than wallboard and wood—a shelter, a lean-to
that was easy to leave behind—was the moment when I
started to hate her for it.

I left my Google search and picked up the phone and
called Vanessa. "Have you heard about that beach bungalow they're selling in a contest?"

"I understand that the owner's lived there for forty-
nine years," Vanessa said. "Her husband just died and
the daughter is moving her up to San Francisco. She
agreed to go so long as she could find the right owner
for her house."

"There's something very cool about it."

"She picked the wrong year though," Vanessa said. "The market's too hot."

"Why should that matter?"

"Did you ever hear of the Dutch Tulip craze?"

"I can't say that I have."

"The richest men in Holland fought over these dirty little root balls that could produce a flower that was just the right red or yellow. Huge fortunes were made and lost, but the thing is that those men couldn't have cared less about the actual flowers. They weren't gardeners. They just liked the art of the deal and the promise of making huge amounts of money in ridiculously short periods of time. We've got the same thing here with houses. People will do anything for the right house."

"Maybe that's exactly why she's doing this right now. To rise above all that."

"How is she going to tell who's just spinning a yarn about loving her house? There's no way to know. Someone told me the other day about this couple who won a bidding war on a house because they convinced the sellers how much they loved the kitchen—how they'd use the two ovens to bake their special holiday cookies and how they'd have other couples over for gourmet dinner parties in which the guests would slice and season the fresh ahi steaks at the big central island right before they were seared. Three weeks after escrow closed, they bulldozed the lot."

"Maybe the bungalow owner has a special bullshit detector," I said.

"You know what I like about you, April? You don't have a cynical bone in your body."

⁓

As if to prove Vanessa's point, I immediately called an editor at *Metropolitan Home*. Without even developing a story pitch, I just picked up the phone and dialed. "There's a house in L.A. being sold by a widow in a contest," I said. "It's an old beach bungalow worth several million dollars. All she wants is three hundred thousand dollars from the right buyer. A buyer with the right soul. It's a great feature story."

"Californians are seriously strange about their real estate," she said.

"*Quirky* was the word I was thinking of."

"Too quirky for us."

"It's got great visuals," I said. "It's a perfectly preserved early Craftsman bungalow standing all alone on a street of McMansions. There are fruit trees all over the yard."

"Try *This Old House*. Or *Sunset*."

"*Sunset* will probably want to scout *my* house. They'd love the glass wall concept. They're not going to do an old beach bungalow."

"And neither are we," she said. "But we're doing a series on the most popular household items of all time. We need someone to talk to Chuck Williams. You interested?"

"You're talking about the Williams-Sonoma Chuck Williams?"

"He's eighty-seven. We need eight hundred words."

"What's the deadline?"

"First week of January."

"Sure," I said, because it's what I always said to keep myself in business, "I can do it."

I drove to the Williams-Sonoma in the mall on the hill in order to soak up the atmosphere. I somehow ignored the fact that it was a week before Christmas and the atmosphere would be chaos. Even in the parking lot I could see the fierce looks on the drivers' faces, the tense set of their jaws. After three trips around the lot, trolling for a spot, I caught the eye of a mom with two young kids in a stroller. She nodded her head toward the next lane over, and I sped around, stopped in the middle of the lane, flipped on my turn signal and waited to claim the spot as my own. I waited ten minutes while the mom opened her minivan and buckled in first one kid, then another. She came around to the back and folded up her stroller, then hoisted it inside. Finally, she got in her seat, buckled up and backed out. I began to move toward the spot, when a man in a silver BMW zipped up from the other side, flew around the minivan and skidded into the empty spot. I pulled up directly behind him and leaned on my horn.

"What?" he asked, leaning out of his car as if he'd done nothing wrong.

"No way," I said. "There is no way. That's my spot."

"Says who?"

"Don't be a jerk," I said. "It's Christmas."

He got back in his car, backed out and vacated the spot. "Merry fucking Christmas," he yelled, as he drove away. I pulled in and turned off the car. I was shaking. A few weeks before, someone had been shot in a mall parking lot. Someone's grandmother. She'd come back to her car, her arms full of bags from Nordstrom, and someone came right up and shot her for the money in her purse. Why had I thought I would be immune?

~

The front windows of Williams-Sonoma displayed KitchenAid mixers in red, yellow, pumpkin and sage, with melamine bowls of matching spatulas arranged like tulips. Even from outside, I could smell apple cider and cinnamon. I stepped in. There was a woman doing a demonstration on how to make English toffee, and people were crammed around her workstation trying to see exactly how she got such an even covering of nuts. People were also lined up at the cash register clutching fluted ceramic pie dishes, sets of copper cookie cutters, coffee cake mixes and French dish towels tied up with cotton bows. I walked along the far wall past the shelves that held vegetable graters, lemon zesters and wooden spoons in every conceivable size and shape. All of it was gorgeous, ready to be wrapped, opened and used to whip up something that would no doubt be delectable.

I selected a pumpkin-colored spatula and took my place in the line.

"Quite a scene," I said to the woman in front of me. She was holding a bright red silicone muffin tray.

"But worth it," she said. "I buy all my gifts here."

"Always muffin trays?" I asked.

"Oh, no, this is for me," she said. "I like to give vinegars and olive oils. The bottles are so pretty."

When it was my turn to pay, I asked the cashier if it had been this hectic all week.

"It's been very busy," she said. "We can hardly keep

most of the items stocked." She looked roughly my age, and I guessed that she had taken this job because her kids no longer needed her and this was the place where she felt most comfortable. Her kids had, perhaps, embarked on a new life on a college campus somewhere and she had embarked on a new life at Williams-Sonoma.

"What do you think makes it so compelling?" I asked, as if the question had just popped into my head.

She answered as if she were reading from the annual report. "We sell quality kitchen products displayed like fine jewelry. I mean, every pot has its place on the shelf, with its handle turned just so. It lets women behave like kids in a candy store."

She wrapped my spatula in tissue paper and tucked it into a green paper bag with twined handles. "Enjoy!" she said.

I took my bag and made my way to the second floor, to Borders, where I could buy a copy of *This Old House.* Near the top of the escalator, I passed by a shop I swore I had never seen before. It was called Soothe Your Soul. There were giant gongs in the window, and wind chimes and a banner announcing that there were great holiday gifts inside. *Soothe Your Soul*. It sounded, in that moment, exactly like what I needed. I walked in.

The small store was filled with the sound of falling water. There were fountains plugged in against three walls. Stones were laid on the ground near the fountains, carved with words like BREATHE, ABUNDANCE and TRUST. There was a musty smell, and as I walked through the store I could discern lavender, sage and something sweet, like ginger. I scanned the bookshelves, wanting to buy each title for its breezy promise of peace, and when I got to the end, I was near the cash register.

"Can I help you?" the woman behind the counter asked. She had long gray hair pulled back in a ponytail and not a lick of makeup on her face. Was she at peace? Did she feel the harmony of the universe? Was the God of her childhood something she still believed in? She didn't look like a woman whose body was patched together, constantly on the verge of flying apart.

I turned toward her to answer—"*I'm just looking*"— and saw a gathering of small, carved Buddhas. They were jade, only about a half inch tall. Some of them seemed to hold things in their hands or over their heads.

I picked one up. He was holding a kind of cup or platter overhead. I could see veins running through the stone. His round belly made him look jolly. I realized that I had no idea who Buddha really was or what he represented. I knew the story of Jesus inside out: Jesus's conception, Jesus's birth, Jesus's parables, Jesus's miracles, Jesus's death. I knew Jesus's story better than I knew my own.

"What does this one mean?" I asked the woman.

"That's the Buddha of long life," she said.

"I'll take it."

"Is it a gift?" she asked. It was testimony to my state of mind that I thought—*What business is it of yours?*—before realizing that she was probably seeking simple information on a box, a bag, a bow, and then realizing, further, that the only Christmas gift I'd purchased was a digital camera for my mother.

"No," I said, trying hard to make sure I sounded pleasant. "It's for me."

"Would you like a book on Buddhism?" she asked. "We have some excellent introductory guides. Some people also like these cards." She pointed to a sturdy little box with a flip-open top and handed it to me, but I didn't want to do anything that smacked of effort. I wanted my prayers to be essential, easy and organic. *Long life*. That was all I felt I could pray for right now—the simple act of breathing in and out over time.

"Just the Buddha is fine," I said.

I paid for the little statue, then slipped it into the pocket of my purse. While I walked through Borders, I reached in three separate times to make sure it was still there. I found the magazine right away, then went to stand in line. It was a long line. Stacked on tables next to us were the books being touted as perfect gifts that holiday season. There was Mitch Albom's new book, *The Five People You'll Meet in Heaven*; a novel called *The Lovely Bones* that I'd been told by three separate people I had to read; *Atkins for Life*; a little red book of advice by Fred Rogers, who had recently died; and Michael Moore's diatribe, *Dude, Where's My Country?* I picked up a copy of the novel, and stepped forward in line. Now I was next to the sale books—a Crock-Pot cookbook, a book of crossword puzzles, a coffee-table book on neon road signs. I picked up a book called *Feng Shui: Harmonizing Your Inner and Outer Space.*

I opened it and flipped to the introduction. "For the ancient Chinese," it said, "luck was not synonymous with chance. Luck was opportunity. Of course, even if presented with opportunity, many of us do not act and grasp it with both hands."

"Next!" the cashier called. I slammed shut the book on feng shui, tossed it back onto the sale table, and made my way past the Mary Engelbreit display to the counter.

The cashier was a young woman with hair that seemed as if it had been dipped in ink. I imagined that she was a seasonal employee. A college student, perhaps, earning money for a trip home. "Busy today, isn't it?" I asked.

"I guess," she said. She swiped my novel across her scanner, shoved it in a bag.

"That's supposed to be an amazing book," I said.

She thrust my receipt toward me to sign. "No returns without a receipt," she said, "and all returns have to be within thirty days."

"OK," I said. "Thanks."

"Next!" she called out.

"Happy Holidays," I said as I walked away, but I knew she hadn't heard me.

⁓

This Old House is a fantastic magazine. It's printed on beautiful, thick paper, for one thing, and on every page you get the feeling that all things are possible. It is possible to clean your gutters, to re-plane a sticky door frame, to scrape off four layers of paint to reveal the original hardwood under the floor of a farmhouse kitchen. For their holiday issue, the magazine had a gift-giving guide featuring laser levels, push-button measuring tapes, and circular saws. The photographs made the tools look as enticing as fine chocolates or cashmere sweaters the color of sorbet. I turned down a page featuring a laser measuring tape that I thought Rick would love, and thought I could probably get one for my brother, as well. I read the column on how to caulk around the windows and lay in extra insulation during the chill of January and pored over a feature story on a hacienda in Arizona that was being restored for a family who had inherited the original property from the wife's great-grandfather, who had been a ranch hand during the Depression.

I was reading about old houses and the people who loved them, but I couldn't get Vanessa's comment out of my head. *You don't have a cynical bone in your body.* That was the way I used to be and it amazed me that the world could see me as unchanged. When the plastic surgeon removed my breast and replaced it with a fake one made from the fat and skin from my tummy, I was only focused on what I'd gained: a breast, a body that was balanced and free of disease. I never concerned myself with what I had lost—my innocence, my faith, the frivolous lightness of being. I had been cancer-free for five years now. That was a joyous landmark, devoutly to be wished, and while I could revel in a good story or in the blessing of being able to witness my daughter growing into such a fine young woman, the fact of the matter was that cancer had made me feel mortal, and it's hard to be optimistic when you feel so damn mortal. It's hard to believe in God, it's hard to feel excited about a new house, it's hard to let your husband love you.

In the beginning, I was grateful and smug, because most of the women in my support group said their husbands were too repulsed to touch them and they were convinced that no one ever would again, except out of pity. Rick, however, never flinched in the face of the wounds I sustained when I lost a breast. He cleaned those wounds, cared for them, then kissed them in a seamless progression of love and desire. But as the years passed and the mammograms came back clean, it began to be more difficult—the whole messy business of love and life.

It's hard to say why this is so, but the further away we got from the event itself, the more tenuous my grip on survival became. I felt more and more mortal as time went by. I felt more and more the risk there was in loving other mortals, in making alliances, in staking a place on this fragile earth. At these times I couldn't stand my husband's touch. My right breast was completely numb because it was completely fake. I appeared balanced and whole and I mostly felt balanced and whole—except when he touched me. He'd put his lips on my left, live, nipple, and all I could feel was the nonresponse of the one on the right. He'd move to the right one and all I could feel was his sense of duty, like a soldier following the protocol he knew to be right. I wanted to yell, "It doesn't work!" but I never did. Was it possible he actually enjoyed it?

As our fourteenth anniversary approached—which was a year and a half ago—guilt overwhelmed me. Rick didn't deserve a wife who had been sick, and he didn't deserve a wife who had grown so cold. I wanted to do something to show him how grateful I was for his compassion and constancy, and what I did was this: I had my fake breast tattooed. The idea came to me when I overheard a conversation where a mother was expressing her outrage that her daughter had gone to a place called Art & Soul. The girl had just waltzed in and gotten a shamrock tattooed on her ankle because her boyfriend was an Irishman. I was taken with that concept—of outrageous spontaneity, of permanent adornment for an audience of just one. I was certain Rick would be taken with it, too.

Not long after the thought first came to me, I was in line at the grocery store behind a small, fit woman with an elaborate dragon tattooed on her shoulder blade. The tail snaked down her arm and the body covered most of the rounded knob of her shoulder. She was wearing a white spaghetti-strap tank, and I could clearly see the whole beast—its tail, its wings, its scales.

"That's beautiful," I ventured, pointing.

She turned her head, and registered no surprise that a slightly heavy, apricot-haired mother wearing plain black flip-flops, a denim skirt that hit below her knees, and an expression of extreme exhaustion, was interested in her tattoo.

"It's Cold Drake Dragon from *Lord of the Rings*," she said. "Erika Stanley did it at Art and Soul. I had to wait six months to get an appointment with her."

"Art and Soul," I repeated. "I've heard of it."

The next day, I drove half an hour on the freeway to the studio on Robertson Boulevard. I was stunned to find that it was more like an art gallery than a sleazy bar. The walls were white and the space was open. There were large, colorful posters on the wall of various tattoos, framed award certificates and row upon row of black binders filled with tattoo designs.

"Can I help you?" a man behind the counter asked. He had heavily gelled hair and a small goatee. I couldn't detect a tattoo anywhere on him.

"I'd like a tattoo," I said. "On my breast. I only have three hours. I want to do it before I lose my nerve."

"Tattoos are permanent art," he said, as if I were a sixteen-year-old rebel. "Are you sure you wouldn't like to take some time to browse through our designs, and then come back when you're certain you're ready? We don't normally recommend tattooing on impulse."

"I'm certain," I said, surprised and reassured by his conservative kindness. "Just nervous."

"Do you know what design you want?"

"A butterfly. Just a small one."

He got up, reached for a binder, flipped it open and revealed a dozen butterfly designs. "That's only the start of what we have, and we can do custom work, too, though that's more expensive and takes longer." The colors of the butterflies were rich and earthy. There were creatures that looked like specimens from a science book and ones that looked as if they'd flown right off the page of a fantasy novel. I didn't want to turn the page and get lost in consideration. I pointed to a blue butterfly about as big as my thumbnail, with radiant flecks of green. You could see the shadow of the wings, which made it look like it was flying, like it could be captured in the mouth of the man who might go to kiss it, and then be swallowed whole.

"That one," I said.

I signed all the waivers and legal agreements, then sat down and read *Details* magazine while I waited for one of the artists to be free. I kept glancing over the top of the pages at a man whose forearm was completely covered in tattoos. There were words and various animals included among the designs, but I couldn't make any of them out. There were so many tattoos that the whole effect was just one of ink. After about fifteen minutes, my name was called.

The man with the goatee led me back to a small room and handed me a black cotton gown.

"Shirt off, bra off," he said. "Leave the opening of the gown to the front. Jerry will be with you in a minute."

He closed the door and I quickly took off my clothes and put on the gown. I thought about how many times

I'd been in a small room in a gown waiting for an expert to come in an do something to my breast—poke it with a needle, squeeze it for an X-ray, cut it, sew it, clean it, measure it, burn it. I was an expert at having things done to my breast. I could whip my clothes off in an instant. I could carry on a conversation as serious as the possibility of life and death or as frivolous as the desirability of having a deep décolletage without giving a thought to the indignity of wearing a thin cotton gown tied loosely across my body. People could poke and prod at any part of my anatomy they were trained to treat and I wouldn't flinch. I wouldn't even blink.

I looked around the little room and noticed a diploma on the wall. Jerry Steiner, it seemed, was a graduate of the Chicago School of Art. While I was still marveling at this fact, Jerry himself walked in and introduced himself. He was a thin man with a tattoo like a braided rope around his left wrist.

"I'm going to numb you up," he said, then stopped because I was shaking my head.

"It's already numb. I had a mastectomy. It's completely fake."

"Ahh," he replied, and the way he said it made me wonder if he knew what a mastectomy even was. Perhaps he thought I had just told him that I'd had breast enhancement surgery. Maybe this was why he acted as if it were nothing. "Well, I'm going to numb you up anyway," he said.

Even after the shots, I could feel the vibration of the machine that punched the needle and a kind of concentrated electric energy on that part of my body. It was uncomfortable. I lay on the table and tried not to move, or even breathe, so as not to disturb Jerry while he worked. When he was done, he instructed me in how to care for the scab that would form over the tattoo, and gave me some paperwork that answered any questions I might have.

I dressed, thanked the man with the goatee and went to pick up Jackie from school.

The butterfly was a pretty design, executed in clear, fine lines, and it floated there on my breast, but much like the breast itself, it didn't feel like mine. I'd done it for Rick. I had to tell him about it to keep him from touching the tattoo, or brushing against it as it healed, but I told him he couldn't see it until I was ready. I dressed in the dark and turned away from him when I pulled on my nightgown. This sent him into a frenzy of desire, which I found more gratifying than anything else; at least I hadn't miscalculated.

I revealed the little piece of art to Rick in a dark Jacuzzi at a swank hotel in La Jolla. We were alone in the pool in the dark. I slipped into the water across from him, slipped the strap off my bathing suit—a standard mother's black one-piece, so tight it was guaranteed to make you look ten pounds thinner—and pulled the fabric down just enough to let him see. He lunged across the pool and traced it with his finger, took my breast in his hand, and bowed his head to kiss it. I slipped out of his grasp and climbed out of the pool. He trailed after me back to our room like a puppy dog.

I thought the jolt of excitement would jolt me, too. I thought there would be an automatic reciprocal reaction—my frank ploy to rouse him bouncing back to rouse me, too—but it didn't work. Even then, when I offered myself to him as a gift, I didn't enjoy having sex with my husband. I *did* it, and my body did what it was supposed to do, but my mind never shut down, never gave in. The whole time, I was wholly conscious—a scarred middle-aged mother at a hotel by the beach navigating the logistics of copulation. There was no moment of abandonment, no moment when I gave myself over to pleasure. I missed Jackie. Even in the very midst of it, I missed Jackie. And with every touch, with every glance, death was in bed with me, too—the death that I didn't die, the death I one day would, the death of all of us, eventually.

$\mathcal{S}$ATURDAY

On Saturday, there were cars lined up all along Pepper Tree Lane—huge cars, taking up a lot of space. They were all silver, white and black, like beasts lined up for slaughter. I parked two blocks away and walked back to the open house, thinking the entire way about love at first sight—love of boys, of bras, of houses.

It makes perfect sense that you could know in an instant that something, or someone, was just right for you. Why not? It's not a skill you have to acquire so much as it is an attribute you possess without effort, like taste. You know in an instant when the tomato you are eating is a perfect example of summer perfection or when a scoop of vanilla ice cream has achieved a divine alchemy. The same is true of love. You look, you see, you experience, and you know. The moment I saw Peg Torrey's beach bungalow, I knew that it had been made for me; setting foot inside was merely confirmation.

The first thing that struck me, when I walked through the extra wide front door, was the perfect proportions of the doorways and hallways, ceilings and walls. They seemed to be designed on a scale for which my own body was the model. They seemed to be calling out for me to come on in, sit down, stay awhile in a place that fits. I stood just inside the door, looking down the main hallway toward the bright bedrooms and the leafy backyard, looking to the left toward the massive pine dining room table and the golden kitchen, and looking to the right into the living room with its barn red walls, and I had the sense that I could have just stood there forever, taking it all in.

By the door, there was a basket of blue protective shoe coverings. I must have looked at them with confusion or disgust, because a kind woman dressed all in black materialized out of nowhere and suggested that if I didn't want to use the booties, I could simply take my shoes off. I nodded. I slipped off my flats and let my feet touch the old cherry hardwood. We'd put bamboo in the house on Vista del Mar—a whitewashed wood, durable, with a modern flair. I hadn't yet walked on it barefoot, but I imagined it was going to be cool. This wood was warm. It felt like the sun-warmed earth. It was red and rich, and it anchored the house to the ground.

"I bet they've used a lot of Murphy's Oil Soap," someone said behind me. I turned to see a stylish woman slipping blue plastic over her sporty Mary Janes.

Besides the floor, there was wood everywhere. The mantel was made of cherry, as were the built-in bookcases on either side of it. There was a window seat capped with a thick cushion covered in a gorgeous blue block print with red piping the color of the walls. A pillow of the same fabric was tossed against the worn leather couch. On the ground in front of the fireplace, there was a black and white cowhide. I stared at that cowhide for the longest time. Who would ever think that such a thing would work? Who would ever make the choice to paint their walls red and throw a cowhide rug on the floor? It was preposterous. It was fabulous.

The pine table in the dining room to the left was huge. Twelve sage green chairs gathered around it with room to spare. The table filled that room. It was easy to imagine kids doing homework on those planks, women sewing Halloween costumes, turkeys being carved, candles being burned, birthday cakes being sliced and served. There was another window seat in the dining room—the mate of the one in the living room on the other side of the door—and two narrow bookshelves had been fitted on either side of it. If you sat on the seat, you would be able to see the ocean out the window—a sliver of water down at the end of the street. Turn the other way, and you'd be gazing at a quilt that hung on the wall, a quilt that clearly told a story. It was a fractured image of a fish. A trout, maybe, with rainbow colors on its belly. At least eight shades of blue fabric formed the stream in which it swam: silks and calicos, batiks and abstracts.

It was so loud and boisterous in the kitchen it sounded

like there was a party in full swing. I stepped down the hallway instead. The walls of the hall were lined with board games that had been frozen in time, framed and hung on the wall. There was a Monopoly game in which someone had hotels on Marvin Gardens and Boardwalk, and someone was clean out of money. There was a Candyland game with a piece suspended forever in the Molasses Swamp. I stopped in front of Clue—Colonel Mustard in the Conservatory with a Lead Pipe had done it—and marveled that someone had thought to preserve their family's joy in this way. I wished it had been me.

The hallway led to the back garden, which was framed by a trellis painted purple and punctuated by a faded yellow market umbrella. A fire pit was surrounded by wrought iron chairs with faded cushions made of a striped fabric that had probably once been really bright. Flagstone steps wound through the grass, back toward a built-in barbecue, and eucalyptus trees marched in stately procession along the back fence, their trunks silvery and ghostlike even in the bright light of day. They reached straight and clean to the sky, throwing off their sharp scent, standing guard. Along the side fence were fruit trees: lemon, lime and avocado. Fruit littered the ground, brown and rotting. I watched as one man yanked a lime off the tree absentmindedly. He was talking to two women. They were standing near the back fence looking toward the house as if it were a kingdom they were about to conquer.

"Mrs. Torrey designed the trellis herself," someone said. I turned to see the woman in the black suit. She had been watching me staring into space. "She and her husband lived here for forty-nine years. They were only the second owners."

"Was she an architect?" I asked.

"No, just a resourceful housewife," the woman said, "which is something of a tradition for the house. The original owner was a librarian. She came out here from the Midwest as a single woman in 1928."

"You must be the seller's agent," I said.

She held out her hand. "Lane McNamara," she said. "Beach Cities Realty."

There were a dozen questions I wanted to ask, but I kept thinking of the woman on the street with the poodles. "Is the owner crazy?" I asked.

Lane laughed, and another woman—much smaller, wearing jeans and expensive European clogs—appeared next to her. It was this woman who answered me.

"My dad's been dead, what? Has it been a whole month?" the clog lady said. "And in that month, my mom has tried to walk into the ocean like Virginia Woolf, she's collected enough sleeping pills from Dad's old colleagues to kill a team of horses, and she's rejected six full-price offers on her house in favor of a contest that's brought a parade of peepers, desperate home buyers, history buffs and newspaper reporters to her front door. What part isn't crazy?"

"She must have really loved him," I said.

"You have no idea," the daughter said, and in the moment she said this, the look on her face instantly changed from combative to angelic. It was as if there was no way she could deny the power of her parents' love.

I turned away.

"I'm sorry for your loss," I mumbled. A real reporter would have kept digging—cornered the daughter for insight on what it was like to grow up in that house, pressed the real estate agent for clues as to what Mrs.

Torrey was looking for. Even a halfway decent reporter would have dropped the names of the publications she'd worked for to whet the appetite of her prey. But I wasn't a real reporter; I was a women's magazine writer. I didn't have it in me to intrude upon these people's lives. I only had it in me to skirt along the surface of a story like a water bug. Standing there by that purple trellis, I knew that any magazine for which I would write about the last beach bungalow would reduce it to its basest elements: five healthy steps to take in the first weeks after losing a spouse; six novel ways to increase traffic at an open house; three unusual ways to sell a house. I suddenly didn't want to have any part of it.

I froze up in the same way I had when *Glamour* magazine sent me to interview Melissa Gilbert at her home in the Hollywood Hills. I was supposed to grill her about what went on behind the scenes when she beat out Victoria Principal to be president of the Screen Actors Guild. But Melissa Gilbert had been Laura Ingalls, with the braids, the freckles, the charming crooked teeth. She had been the girl who wandered off on a rocky ridge and met God, and who dipped Nellie Olson's braids in ink right in plain sight of the teacher. I couldn't grill her. Even though she was an adult sitting in front of me expecting to be grilled, I couldn't do it. I limped through a few sad questions about the vote, then pretty much sat there and gawked at the green eyes and red hair.

The same thing happened in the beach bungalow. I had my chance, but I took a step backward and walked away.

As I made my way back to the front of the house, I heard a woman say to her husband, "He *died* in that room, Bruce. I asked the Realtor point-blank and he *died* there. Cancer. She said it was his *choice*—to die in bed at home. I, for one, am not living in a house with that kind of legacy."

A house with that kind of legacy was exactly what I longed for—a house whose walls had stories to tell. I'd never been able to pinpoint it in all the endless discussions Rick and I had while we were building our house on the hill. We kept talking about the configuration of the kitchen cabinets and how the traffic would flow around the furniture and where we would put the piano and what kind of shower door was easiest to clean, but we had no language to talk about legacy. There is no legacy when everything is brand-new, and there's no legacy when you move from place to place the way I had for my entire childhood. I wanted walls that talked. I'd only known them once, in the house my grandmother had built on the shores of Squam Lake in New Hampshire.

It was a cottage, really, but it was the place where I'd learned to swim on a plastic foam dolphin, and the place where I'd sat and shelled peas on the porch. My grandfather taught me to play cards on a table he'd set up in the living room and my grandmother taught me to play the piano on an instrument that was so out of place in that cottage as to be laughable. The centerpiece of the whole house was the fireplace. It was made of stone that local men had hauled up from the mouth of the river—smooth river rock in shades of brown and gray. My grandfather died suddenly of a stroke back at the big house in Philadelphia and never even got to say good-bye, but my grandma knew she was dying, and she orchestrated the whole thing. She asked to be brought to the cottage so she could die in front of the fireplace, where it was always warm and there was always something to see out the window. They shoved the piano aside and set up a hospital bed, and waited for the cancer to march through her body.

It had started in her breast, migrated to her lungs and her liver and found a beachhead in her brain. I was only eleven and I had only known storybook deaths up until that time—deaths that happened either off-stage or in peaceful silence. Gram's death was nothing like those. She was old, for one thing—eighty-seven. One by one, over the last several years, she'd had to stop doing the things she used to be able to do. At first it was pleasures, like walks in the woods, and then it was complexities, like paying bills. As the cancer consumed her, it came down to the necessities of daily life. She lost the ability to put together a meal, to drive her old blue Cadillac. It took her so long to button her sweater that she could no longer make it to church on Sunday mornings. The only thing she was able to do, in the end, was to die where she wanted to die. Toward the very end, her breathing became ragged and slow, and the pain she felt was so awful it made everyone else in the room hurt, too. My mom didn't have much choice but to let me be part of it.

It was summer and the cottage was small. We sat with Gram, rubbing Vaseline on her lips, holding her hand. We didn't want her to be alone when she drew her last breath, but she had other ideas. She died in the middle of the night, when the fire was out, and no one was sitting beside her.

⁓

When I got home from the open house, Jackie came at me the moment I walked in the door.

"Can I go to church with Max tomorrow?" she asked.

"Church?" I repeated, lamely.

"He goes to the Unitarian Universalist church up on Montemalaga."

Tomorrow was the children's Christmas pageant. There would be a donkey. Someone would speak the lines, *Do not be afraid, I bring you tidings of great joy,* and we would sing "O Little Town of Bethlehem." I looked at Rick, who was sitting on the couch folding laundry and watching a football game. "Did you ask Daddy?" I asked.

"He said to ask you," Jackie said. "Max says they read

from the Bible, the Koran and the Torah, and a few Sundays ago, the sermon was based on a John Irving novel. Don't you love that?"

I wondered if the novel had been *A Prayer for Owen Meany* or *The Cider House Rules*. I could imagine sermons on both books that would be quite powerful— something about the nature of accident, something about the rule of the law versus the spirit of it. "Is Max your boyfriend, then?" I asked, as casually as I was able.

Jackie smiled. "It was official on December fourth," she said.

When she was in fourth grade, a boy she liked gave her a pink plastic heart necklace on Valentine's Day. She was mortified at his audacity and vowed never to speak to him again. It was important that everyone know this. She sealed the necklace in an envelope and had her best friend, Karen, ceremoniously hand it to him in the middle of the playground. He apparently took the envelope and flipped it into the trash can on his way to play basketball, no longer an official boyfriend. But what, in the lexicon of high school, did "official" mean? Had the boy with the blond hair given her a token of his affection that she deigned, this time, to keep? Was it merely a mutual acknowledgment that they liked each other? Or was it just that they decided to hang out together, eat lunch together, go to each other's sporting events?

"Oh," I said, feeling like an idiot. "Official. That's great." She had asked for something of me and had given me something in return. The chance to go to church with the boy she liked for inside information about the boy. It seemed like a fair deal. "I don't see any reason why you can't go to church with him," I said.

Jackie threw her arms around me. "Thanks, Mom!" she said.

"I expect to meet this boy before you go on a date with him," Rick said from the couch. "And church counts."

Jackie disappeared into her room, sealed off from us by her iPod earplugs. We'd given her the iPod last Christmas. It was the only thing she'd asked for—that, and the requisite dog that she had never received. Over the years, her dog requests had become more specific: *a spaniel poodle mix; a rescue dog named Sam who'll be ready at the Redondo shelter in four weeks; a five-year-old pug named Peanut that the Krolls' friends found without tags in the Village and who they say they're going to turn in if no one takes him this week.* This year, she hadn't even bothered with a list. She was getting a new room in a new house that would be the house she left behind when she went away to college and would be the house she came back to when she came home. She was getting the chance to live in a modern vision her dad had created for her mom when it was unclear whether or not her mom was even going to live.

I sat on the couch next to Rick. We were planning on leaving that couch on the curb when we moved into the new house. It was Santa Fe plaid. It had been the first big piece of furniture we'd bought together, with money my parents gave us for our wedding. It had been on sale for $350 (a floor sample) and we were thrilled at our great good fortune when we found it. We hauled it home in Rick's pickup truck and muscled it through the door of our little duplex—the duplex we traded for a nine-hundred-square-foot starter home in North Redondo Beach, which we then traded for the ranch house on Vista del Mar, which we had gutted nine months ago to build a three-story modern mansion with sweeping views of the sea because Rick had built dozens of beautiful custom homes in this town, and it was our turn, now, to show the world through the quality of his craftsmanship and the creativity of our design that we had made it.

"I saw a house today." I could feel my heart beating against my collarbone. It sounded like a drum.

"A house?"

"An old beach bungalow down on Pepper Tree Lane. This old lady is selling it in a contest and I went to the open house."

Rick folded a towel. "You're writing about it?"

"Yeah," I said, the lie coming without a single hitch. "But the thing that was weird is I could picture us living there."

"Sweetie," he said, setting the towel down and turning to face me. He put his hands on my shoulders. "You need to stop feeling nervous about the new house. Everything's going to come together in the end, I promise. I ordered the paint today and Ruben's starting on doorknobs tomorrow. We're so close to the end. We're going to be in for Christmas. It's going to be perfect."

"Remember how I said the other day that I thought I'd seen a ghost?" I asked.

Rick just stared at me.

"There's something about the house. I'm not sure I want to live there."

"We can paint the bathroom blue if it means that much to you," Rick said.

"The bathroom's fine."

"Then what is it?" Rick asked. He raised his arms as he said this and let them slap back down on his thighs. "Just tell me what you want and I can make it happen. You want me to move the whole damn bathroom? I can do anything if you just tell me what will make you happy."

I moved a pile of just-folded jeans onto the coffee table. The football game was still going on, the dull buzz of the crowd.

"You know how they say that cancer changes you?" I said. "I've been wondering the whole time what that means because I don't feel any different than I did before. I actually feel worse, to tell you the truth. We lived through all that. We were so young, Rick. It was so awful. And look at us. I have a brand-new body, we have a brand-new house, but do we even like each other anymore? Are we any better off?"

"So that's what this is about?" he asked quietly.

Tears started to roll down my cheeks. "I know it sounds stupid," I said, "but I never stopped thinking I was going to die. I know you wanted this house to be a kind of fortress against the possibility of that, but I never stopped thinking I was going to die."

He leaned over to me, then, and took me in his arms. I wanted to let my weight fall against his, to let myself melt into him. It felt exactly the way it had when I first met him and we couldn't, physically, stay away from each other. I turned my shoulder toward him and could feel his chest, his thighs against mine. All I would have had to do to set our lovemaking in motion was to raise my chin. I lifted my eyes, and in the next instant, he was kissing me. I opened my mouth to welcome him—just as Jackie stepped out of her bedroom.

I pulled away.

"What's for dinner?" she asked.

"Your mom and I are going out with Vanessa and CJ," Rick said.

"We are?" I asked.

"Vanessa twisted my arm," he said, clearly pleased that he allowed it to be twisted. "We're going to the golf club."

"What's the occasion?" Jackie asked.

"A clean mammogram," I said. "Five years."

Jackie came over to where we were sitting on the couch and flung her long, lean body across our laps, and her arms around my neck. "That's awesome, Mom," she said, and kissed me on the cheek. She smelled like mangoes, from her shampoo. She was surprisingly heavy in my lap, and her hair—the same apricot color as mine, but longer and straighter, the hair I'd always wanted—tickled my arm where it brushed against my skin. "I'm so glad you didn't die."

I laughed. "I'm glad I didn't die, too."

She kissed me again, then Rick tickled her feet and she squealed and got up and went into the kitchen to find something to eat.

I knew exactly what I was supposed to wear if I wanted to look polished and put together—something in a fall shade to complement my reddish hair, something with a wide neckline to emphasize my strong shoulders. Having been bathed in the wisdom of women's magazines my whole adult life, I could reel off the best ways to apply eye shadow, the best shoes to wear with a pair of pencil pants, a dozen different ways to camouflage an extra ten pounds, but the truth was that knowing how to dress was completely different from being able to do it. Most days, I wore the same pair of jeans and a T-shirt, but that was hardly going to work for a dinner at Donald Trump's new golf course. The chairs in the restaurant were heavy brocade. The drapes that framed the ocean view were deep blue velvet.

I pulled out a pair of black pants and a red silk knit sweater I'd worn for Christmas parties for at least eight years. They were a uniform, a safe bet. The only thing that would add any pizzaz whatsoever would be accesso-

ries. Scarves, shoes, bracelets, necklaces, earrings, belts—
the list of things that could bring salvation were endless.
I picked up two pairs of earrings and went and knocked
on Jackie's door.

"Yeah?" she asked, ear buds still in her ears.

"Which ones, do you think?" I asked, holding up the
earrings.

She pulled the ear plugs out. "I'd definitely go with
the gold," she said, in a voice that was too loud for the
real world but just perfect for me.

⁓

We had an appetizer of walnut and shrimp sushi and
California rolls made with crab that had been flown in
from Maryland. Rick ordered warm sake, which we
both love. For dinner, we had pecan-crusted salmon with
baby bok choi and for dessert, there were three kinds of
crème brulee. Rick ordered a bottle of champagne and
raised his glass to make a toast. "To five great years," he
said. He leaned down to kiss me and presented me with

a blue Tiffany box. Inside was a silver heart-shaped key ring with a key to the new house, and a small card that said, "Here's to forever."

"Here, here," CJ said, and drank another sip of champagne.

I squeezed Rick's hand and kissed it. "Thank you, sweetie," I said. He looked at me and winked.

Vanessa produced a small white oblong box.

"What's this?" I asked.

"Just a little something," she said.

It was a gift certificate from a spa that had recently opened in the Village. On a line at the bottom of the coupon were the words "Energy Healer: One Session." Vanessa was a connoisseur of healing treatments. She'd had massages in red rock canyons and pedicures designed to cure every ill known to the foot. She'd had people manipulate the bones in her skull and wrap her entire body in seaweed. Some people thought that there was a pill or a prayer to heal every ill, some people turned to shopping or to drink, but Vanessa thought anything could be made better with a treatment at a spa.

"What magical powers will this bring me?" I asked.

"It will help you stay calm through the big move. I booked you an appointment for Monday."

"Calm sounds good," I said.

"Plus," Vanessa said, "it will ignite your sexual energy."

"Oh, la la!" CJ said.

I slapped his forearm.

"Ouch," CJ said. "She could do some serious damage with that right hook."

"Don't I know it," said Rick.

"No need to have any security guards with her around," CJ went on.

"Or *Ghostbusters*," Rick said.

"Halloween is long past, buddy," CJ said. "You're good with the ghosts."

Rick drained his glass. "April thinks there's something wrong with the house. Evil spirits, that kind of thing."

"I didn't say that," I said.

"It's just the bathroom wall color she doesn't like," Vanessa said.

"That's not true, either," I said, my voice getting higher pitched.

"She's fantasizing about another house," Rick said.

Something about the way my husband said the word *fantasizing* made my belly go cold. Was Rick having an affair? Is that why he had remained so cheerful through all these months when we'd barely touched each other? I scanned my mind for any suspicious comments, any unexplained late-night meetings. An image flashed through my mind of Rick in bed with another woman—a faceless woman, but with dark hair and smooth skin, and hunger in every move she made. Anger welled up in me, as if I'd caught him with his pants down.

"Rick, that's not fair," I growled.

"But it's true," he said, and then turned his face toward CJ. "She keeps talking about some house down by the beach."

"She's writing about that house," Vanessa said. "It's the house from the contest."

I thought of what it had been like to walk through the front door of the beach bungalow, confronted suddenly with the trellis, the trees and the fireplace that was so much like my grandmother's. I thought about how often I had wished that my mother hadn't sold Gram's cottage by the lake. I could swim all the way across that lake, from her dock to the dock of the boys' camp on the other side. There were blueberries to pick on the old dirt road and thick novels on the shelf in the den, and even though it made no sense whatsoever to have a grand piano in a house in the woods, Gram had one. That house had a presence to it that, had I been older, I would have fought to keep. "I'm not writing about it," I said. "That was a lie."

There was silence at the table, even from CJ, whose face was flushed with drink. Even he could tell that some line had been crossed.

"You lied to me?" Vanessa said.

Rick sat back in his chair and crossed his arms in front of his body. "So you're saying that you went to that open house because you actually want a different house?"

I shook my head. "I didn't go looking for a different house," I said. "It just happened."

"This is ridiculous," Rick spat, and turned his body, slightly, toward the thick curtains on the window beside us.

"I know you want our house to save me," I said

quietly, "to be a fortress against anything bad ever happening again, but I don't think I believe a house can do that. I don't think anything can do that."

No one said anything. CJ just kept staring at his glass of champagne, Vanessa was looking at Rick and Rick was looking out the window as if he were watching Tiger Woods teeing off the first green and didn't want to miss a second of the swing.

"Who said anything about being saved?" Rick asked.

"You didn't have to say it," I said.

"Guys," Vanessa said. "Time out. This is supposed to be a party. Come on. Let's finish our champagne."

We sipped our drinks, but the evening was clearly over.

⌒

When we got home, I slipped out of my clothes, got into bed, turned away from Rick and quickly closed my eyes as if I couldn't possibly stay awake another minute.

Sunday

When I woke up, Rick was gone from the bed. He was showered and dressed and sitting at the kitchen counter reading the sports page.

"Do you want some eggs?" I asked.

"I already ate," he said.

I nodded and poked my head into Jackie's room. She was leaning close to the mirrored closet doors and brushing mascara onto her eyelashes. "Do you want some eggs?"

"Already ate," she said. She glanced at my flannel pajamas. "Max will be here soon," she said.

It seemed too much trouble to make eggs just for myself. I put two slices of toast in the toaster and heated water for tea. I stood at the sink with my back to Rick and ate so fast it seemed like I wasn't even chewing.

"Mom?" Jackie said from her doorway. She was staring at my wild hair and my pajamas, "It's eight forty-five."

I tossed my crusts in the garbage, dashed to the shower, threw on a black skirt and a white blouse, dried my hair and came out just as Max knocked on the door.

Jackie let him in and introduced us. He held out his hand to shake mine, and I felt instantly nervous, which seemed utterly unfair. Wasn't he supposed to be the one whose hands were sweaty?

"Your church sounds interesting," Rick said. "Jackie told us a little about it."

Max nodded. "It's pretty cool."

"Have you been going there long?"

"Pretty much all my life," he said, "but I don't go that often anymore because of swimming."

"Max swims butterfly," Jackie said. "He's going to nationals in the spring."

"Good for you," Rick said.

"Congratulations," I added.

"We better go," Max said, glancing at Jackie. He reached out his hand first to Rick, then to me. "It was nice to meet you."

"Nice to meet you, too," I said.

As they walked out the door, I saw Jackie take his hand.

I wanted to tell Rick that I was sorry I'd needled him at dinner last night, and I was sorry about what I felt about the bungalow, and sorry that I hadn't said more than two words to the boy that Jackie brought home, but Rick went to brush his teeth, and then he stood by the door jingling his car keys, saying that it was time to go in a voice that was still brittle with anger.

We rode to church in total silence.

⟿

We belonged to an Episcopal church that was tucked into a grove of eucalyptus trees in a small canyon that I always imagined to be the exact spot where Redondo

Beach, the surf town, gave way to Palos Verdes, the hilly home of doctors and Hollywood lawyers. All the towns in the South Bay were crammed together so that you were never really sure where one began and another ended, but the Redondo–Palos Verdes border felt like a line of demarcation. The curve of beach melted into crumbling cliffs, the hills rose up behind them, and the Palos Verdes Peninsula began its audacious jut out into the sea. The Beach Boys sang about Redondo Beach. It was one of the hot spots you'd hit on your endless summer surfing safari, a place of leisure and delight. But it was from the hills of Palos Verdes that you could view it all: the palm trees silhouetted against the sunset, the crescent of sand wrapping around the Santa Monica bay, the spread of lights across the L.A. basin.

Saint Francis Episcopal Church stood like a sentinel on the road leading up to those lofty views. Rick had been baptized in the original chapel and later served as an altar boy there. He'd kissed a girl named Patti Patterson in the choir stalls of the new sanctuary building one Easter morning in eighth grade. I'd done all those same things, too—except the kissing—at a Methodist church in Houston, Texas. Far from feeling like a compromise, adopting Rick's church and religion felt like a gift I was giving to our marriage. In the beginning I kept noting the differences between the two services: where people prayed or didn't pray, how they kneeled or didn't kneel. After a few years, I stopped paying attention.

On Sunday, I focused on the purple candles on the Advent wreath and tried to feel some connection to God as I sang the familiar hymns and listened to the familiar prayers, but nothing was familiar because Jackie wasn't there and anger still hung in the air around us. During the opening prayers, I tried to focus on the words, but all I could think about was the way Jackie had grabbed Max's hand. During Communion, I tried to pray for the soldiers who had just pulled Saddam Hussein from a hole in the ground and I tried to feel grateful for the simple fact of being able to sit in church on Sunday morning and not worry that I would be shot. My head, however, was filled with an image of the house on Pepper Tree Lane.

The gospel reading and sermon that day were taken over by the pageant. Mary, Joseph, the innkeeper and assorted shepherds and lambs assembled at the back of the church. You could hear them shuffling and whispering, jockeying for position. The real Mary was purported to be a shy young thing, obedient and respectful of the law, but it was a coup to be chosen to play Mary at Saint Francis Palos Verdes, so it was usually a rather pushy girl who got the part—someone with a loud voice and a mother who was capable of spinning light blue silk into a fetching robe. The lights dimmed and a young girl, about twelve, came out and sat down at a piano that had been rolled into the sanctuary for the occasion. She was wearing a black velvet dress with a wide red ribbon around her waist, and her black hair was slicked back in a bun. She smiled and struck the first chord of "Once in Royal David's City."

Mary came up the aisle, the angel Gabriel followed, Joseph came and gave his travel plans, the shepherds who watched their flock were amazed by the star in the sky, but I never took my eyes off the piano-playing girl. I played piano for eight years as a child and I used to love wearing a beautiful dress onstage. It was a thrill to play Chopin, to hit all the notes, to lose myself in the music in front of the audience of adoring parents, but it was all made even better by a great dress and patent leather shoes. It was the clothes that made all the students stand up straighter and walk with a lighter step. My teacher Mrs. K believed in renting an auditorium with a real stage and a grand piano for the recitals, and she insisted on the formal dress. "So you'll know what it's like to play Carnegie Hall," she used to say.

I'd wait in the wings, craning my neck to see if I could see my mom, and if I was lucky that night, my dad. I wanted to memorize where they were sitting so that when I clip-clopped out onto the stage in my shiny shoes and sat on the black bench to play, I wouldn't have to look to know exactly where they were sitting.

My parents never yelled "Brava!" the way some parents did, and they never had a red rose or a little bouquet of flowers for me. My mom would sit and clap until everyone else stopped clapping, and if my dad was there, he would clap three or four times, but that was enough. It was everything. It was all I needed to decide that being onstage was going to be my life. I switched to singing in junior high because the kids who were nice to me in the new school in our new town were in the choir. Whenever my dad wasn't home, I went around the house rehearsing every song to obsessive perfection and became so confident in my voice that in my sophomore year in high school, I landed the role of Cinderella. Those Rogers and Hammerstein songs about love and loneliness and possibility helped me nurture illusions of a singing career until one day at the start of my senior year when my mother took me to hear Kathleen Battle sing.

Ms. Battle was giving a master class at the College Conservatory of Music, and the concert was part of her appearance. She sang from *Aida*, *Don Giovanni* and *The Marriage of Figaro*. From the moment she walked onstage, I was smitten. The unmistakable sweep and grandeur of celebrity clung to everything about her—her hair, her skin, her black top with the wide scoop neck— but it was her voice that devastated me. That magnificent voice. I watched her waltz onstage, saw her open her mouth and heard the sound that came out. I wept, it was so beautiful. And I wept because I knew that she belonged onstage in a way I never had and never would.

She owned it. She came alive on it. She told amusing anecdotes between songs and offered to sign the students' sheet music after she was finished. All the college students lined up to get her autograph, and as I watched them jostle for position, and heard them flatter her with their overenthusiastic praise, I felt utterly deflated. I was utterly destroyed by her talent, and I sometimes wonder if that wasn't the thing my mother had in mind in bringing me there that night.

I signed up for stage crew for the spring musical and when the high school counselors asked me what I was thinking about studying in college, I did not say piano and I did not say singing. I said English. I said I wanted to teach English.

～

When a young mother from the church slipped baby Jesus into the arms of the waiting Mary, I wasn't the only one in the congregation with tears streaming down my face, but I was probably one of the few who thought the piano player had stolen the show.

After church, Rick went on a run down to the beach. I paced around the apartment for a few minutes, picking up and setting down the paper, before I grabbed my purse and got in the car.

I drove first to the twenty-by-thirty foot storage garage where most of our belongings were stacked in boxes against the cinderblock walls. In a large pocket left near the front of the space was the grand piano that had dominated my grandmother's living room. It was a Bösendorfer 170 in high polish ebony. She had left it to me in her will because she knew I loved it. I loved the way it looked like a giant black bird taking flight; I loved the way it sounded, with its magnificent range of tone; and I loved the hours we had sat together in front of it, when she had taught me to play.

My mother sold the house in New Hampshire after my grandmother died. We were living at that point in Houston, and it seemed too far to come to a cottage on a lake. She sold the house and the unwanted odd bits of china and wool coats with holes where the moths had gotten to them. She kept the silver and some paintings, and she had the piano shipped out to us. I'd already been taking lessons for two years by that point, practicing on a Baldwin spinet we'd bought from a neighbor whose kids had outgrown it. Switching to the Bösendorfer was like inheriting a whole country.

I couldn't sleep for the first week we had it in our house. I'd awake in the middle of the night and sneak out just to make sure it was still there, massive and shining in the dark. I'd awake early in the morning, touching the keys without depressing them so as not to wake my parents.

It frightened me, in a way, having my dead grandmother's piano in my house and knowing that it was mine. But I loved being frightened in that way. The piano stayed with my family while I went to college, while I worked as an elementary school teacher after graduation, and while Rick and I were living in our first tiny condo. As soon as we moved into a house big enough for a grand piano—the original ranch house at Vista del Mar—I had it shipped to me. It took up way too much space in our living room, I almost never had time to play and Jackie never showed any interest in doing anything other than banging on the keys, but I loved having it with me all the same.

When it came time to move our belongings out of Vista del Mar for the remodel, the movers unscrewed the legs on the piano, then wrapped all the pieces in bubble wrap. They stood the main box on its side with the keyboard running from floor to ceiling, silenced under all that plastic. I took my car key and carefully sliced away the tape that held the bubble wrap. Crouching down, leaning sideways, I played the opening phrase of Bach's Two-Part Invention, the one in F minor, which I'd played at my first big recital. I wanted to hear the sadness out loud that I felt so silently in my bones.

⁓

I locked the piano behind the corrugated door, then drove up the hill to the mall. I walked past the beguiling smells of Williams-Sonoma's food demonstrations and straight to Soothe Your Soul, where I walked the aisles and looked—at books, at Buddhas, at beads. I stuck my finger into the falling sheet of water that poured from a fountain at the front of the store because if Jackie had been with me, she would have done the same thing the moment she walked through the door. I finally stopped in front of the jewelry case and asked the cashier if I could look at something inside. She took out a necklace made of sterling silver. The chain was made of long links that looked like tiny twigs with hooks at each end. In the center of the chain hung a square charm, and on the charm perched a dove. I turned it over. Engraved on the back of the charm was one word: *peace*.

"That's from a series the artist calls his Soul series," the cashier said. She was the same woman who'd sold me the Buddha. I could tell that she recognized me; something about the way she spoke included an acknowledgment of my having been in that store before, of her having helped me. I felt an odd affection for her.

"I always wonder if an artist who makes something like this is searching for peace or if she's already found it and the art is her way of passing it along," I said.

She shrugged. "I think it amounts to the same thing."

"How so?" I asked.

"Just that everyone is searching for peace, or seeking to pass it along, sometimes both at the same time, or both on the same day. No one ever gets to stop and be done with it. We're all in the mix, all the time. Artists have just figured out a way to make beauty out of the chaos."

I nodded. "I'd like one," I said.

"Would you like it gift-wrapped?"

"No, thanks," I said. "It's for me." While the shopkeeper rang up my purchase, I felt the familiar, strange affliction of wanting to tell every stranger my news. It had first struck me right after I was diagnosed. I told my news to the librarian at Jackie's school, an assistant editor at a new magazine in New York, and the pharmacist at Rite Aid. Anyone who asked how I was doing wasn't going to hear that I was fine. I wasn't fine. I had cancer. It was a relief, in a way, when my hair fell out because I could step outside and my head would be a neon sign. "I just celebrated my five-year cancer-free anniversary," I said, "and this is what I think I'd like to mark the occasion."

The shopkeeper smiled—a lovely, tolerant smile. "Congratulations," she said. "I can't think of a better gift you could give yourself."

I put my wallet in my purse, took the chain from her hand. "Well, actually," I said, "I was thinking about buying a new house."

She laughed. "Why not?" she said, and lifted her hand in a formal flourish.

Why not? Because I could do it, and it could all be for nothing. I could get inside that red living room with the Catalina tile fireplace, inhabit that perfectly proportioned space, and it could make no difference whatsoever. I would still be mortal, I would still be me. Plus there would be leaks in the plumbing and walls in the wrong places and floors that needed to be refinished. It could, in the end, just be wallboard and wood.

"You know what?" I said, turning back to the cabinet with the necklaces, "I'll take another one. And there's no need for a box."

⁓

After I paid, I went out to the car. I hooked one of the necklaces around my own neck, then wrote a note on a piece of paper from a plumbing supply store:

Mrs. Torrey,

I felt something in your house I hadn't felt in a very long time, and the only word I can think to describe it is peace. *I felt peace in your house. Feeling it in your house made me see that maybe peace is somewhere inside me, too. I wanted to thank you for that, and pray that you find it, too.*

April Newton

I drove down the hill and parked across the street from the bungalow, then sat there fiddling with the charm around my neck. I finally got out, crossed the street, opened the gate and walked up to the front door. I reached out and slipped the chain around the doorknob, then stood there a minute to fold the note around the chain. I finally turned, took a step down to the sidewalk, glanced up—and saw Rick standing on the other side of the gate with a flier in his hand.

We always see the people we love at such close range—across bedrooms and kitchen counters. It was a shock to see him standing there in someone else's yard, like a stranger who had just happened by. He was an attractive man with a friendly, open face. His skin was wet with sweat and his shirt clung to his chest. If I hadn't known him, I might have smiled at him. We might have exchanged a few pleasantries. Perhaps, if the moment was right, we would have had a conversation where we made an actual connection, like the one I'd just had with the cashier at the store. But then we would pass out of each other's lives, back into the small circle of people whom we love but don't necessarily see.

Rick raised his free hand and waved sheepishly at me. I waved back and met him at the gate.

"What did you leave?" he asked.

I blushed and looked at the ground. "Just a note," I said. I waited a split second to see if the half-truth would stand on its own but it wouldn't. "And a necklace like this one," I said. "They're talismans of peace." I expected him to tease me, or to ask how on earth I had come to be the owner of a pair of necklaces that were talismans of peace. We were, after all, still in the middle of a fight. Instead he nodded, as if, out of all the choices of things to bring the owner of a house I had fallen in love with instead of the one he had built, a necklace like mine had been a good one.

"So you've met the owner?" he asked and glanced at the flier in his hands. "Peg Torrey?"

"You learn a lot about her just by walking through the house," I said. "She likes games and bright colors. There's this huge fireplace in the living room made of the most gorgeous Catalina tile—reds and oranges. It reminds me of Gram's."

"I'm sorry about last night," Rick said. "I shouldn't have teased you."

"I'm sorry about the house. Or the houses. I mean, I'm sorry about what I said about our house. And I'm sorry about this one. I didn't plan on it. I never intended it to happen."

"You have to admit that this is a bit odd." He swept his arm across Peg Torrey's lawn and front porch, the front door and the transom windows with the arts-and-crafts flowers.

"Haven't you ever thought about living in another house—about what our lives would be like if we picked up and moved to a colonial in Boston or an adobe in Santa Fe or even just another house on another part of the hill? Don't you ever just fantasize?"

I hadn't intended to use that word—the same word Rick had used the night before in the restaurant when he'd all but said that dreams about houses were as illicit as dreams of flesh—but I did, and in response, Rick laughed. It was a sickening sound like an inside joke you're not in on.

"Sure I fantasize," he said. It was clear that he wasn't talking about houses anymore.

"Are you sleeping with someone else?" I blurted.

"I fantasize," he said coolly, "but I don't act on it."

My mind reeled. I thought of my mother, silently waiting all those years for my dad to come back from Cincinnati or Chicago or Atlanta after a weekend leadership conference or sales meeting or incentive trip, waiting and knowing the whole time that he was with someone else. She would smile when he returned, ask how his trip was, serve a steak, a potato and beer in front of the TV if there was a game on. How could she have done it?

"You've thought about sleeping with other women?"

Rick shrugged. He had lush, curly hair, and on that day he was in need of a haircut. There was a place just behind his ear where his curls hit the soft skin of his neck, and I could see those curls, plastered against his sweaty skin. The thought skittered across my mind that I might never touch that place on his neck again. It was the corollary to a thought I had often had over the years when, at a party or one of Jackie's sporting events, he'd slip his hand from the small of my back onto the rounded curve of my bottom, or place a hand around the knob of my bare shoulder in a gesture that was intimate and proprietary. He was allowed to touch me in those ways in public because I was his wife. The rules allowed for it. I loved that sense of privilege, and it had been so long since I'd felt it.

"All guys think about it," he said.

"So what stopped you? Why didn't you?" I expected that he'd say something vague about guilt or it just not being right. He was, after all, the kind of guy who wouldn't cross a double yellow line even if there wasn't another car in sight.

"I love you," he said, then smiled a wry, sideways smile, "and I thought that things would get better when we got into the house."

So that was the rub. I was thinking that things would fall apart in that house, and he was thinking that things would get better.

The longest-running feature in an American consumer magazine is the *Ladies' Home Journal* column, "Can This Marriage Be Saved?" It's been a regular part of the magazine for fifty years. A man and a woman take turns saying what's wrong in their relationship and then a counselor comes in to give her advice on what, if anything, they can do to move forward. People love it because it forces them to see all sides of a story in a three-page spread. Even without the astute therapist, I could see that ours was a marriage that could be saved. We both had faith in wallboard and wood to transform a life, it was just that our faith took a different shape.

"It's a beautiful house," I said. "It's one of your best."

"The movers come in two days."

"So we'll move, then," I said.

"What about the talisman of peace?"

I fingered my necklace. The cool hardness of the little square felt comforting. I could feel the place on the back where the word *peace* was carved into the metal. "We'll just have to see."

Rick folded up the flier and slipped it into the pocket of his running shorts.

"Can I have a ride home?" he asked.

We walked to the car, but before we even got our seat belts buckled, my cell phone rang. It was Jackie, asking if she could stay at Max's house and study.

"Are his parents home?" I asked.

"Yeah," she said. "Do you want to talk to them?"

"I have to," I said. "It's my job."

A woman came on the line and said, "Hello? April? I'm Wendy Callahan, Max's mom."

"Nice to meet you, Wendy. Are you sure it's OK for Jackie to stay longer? I don't want her to intrude on your Sunday."

"It's no intrusion," Wendy said. "We're delighted to have her."

"And you'll be home the whole time?" I asked, feeling like an actress reading a script.

"Absolutely," Wendy said, saying the lines of her script back to me in perfect time.

When I hung up, I turned to Rick. "Do you ever get the feeling that Jackie's already gone?" I asked. "I thought we got her for another year and a half, but we don't really have her at all, do we?"

"She's supposed to be gone," Rick said. "If she wasn't gone, there'd be something wrong."

I took a huge gulp of air and let it all the way out. "Don't you ever get tired of being so damn reasonable? Don't you ever just want to do something that makes no sense whatsoever?"

Rick looked at me and in a voice that was dead serious, he said, "No."

We spent the afternoon packing, exchanging excruciatingly polite questions and answers about where we were putting the linens and whether we thought we should leave out any pots to cook for the next few nights or if Baja Fresh would be nourishment enough. We exchanged masking tape and Sharpie pens as the stacks of boxes in the apartment grew like walls around us. At one point, Rick came and stood in the doorway of the bedroom, where I was packing up shoes.

"Do we have anything for Jackie for Christmas?" he asked.

"I was thinking we could do an extreme makeover in her new room—new bedspread, a new beanbag, maybe a desk. I've got stuff scouted out at IKEA."

Rick nodded. "That sounds good." He paused several moments before talking again. "And what about you?" he asked. "What do you want?"

I thought of a thousand things to say before I decided on the simplest version of the truth. "Surprise me," I said.

Late in the day, I went over to the house with the few remaining plants we had kept alive in the apartment. I slowed when I got to the driveway and saw Lucy, the young Mexican woman Rick used for his construction cleaning. She swept up the sawdust, scrubbed the new tile and mopped the floors of the multimillion dollar houses Rick built all over the South Bay. Sometimes other women worked with her—women with brown skin and open faces—but often, she worked alone. She was reaching into her little pickup truck to set down her bucket of cleaning supplies, and the moment I saw her, she saw me. She smiled and waved—the boss's wife.

"All done!" she called. "So now you can be moving in."

"Thank you, Lucy," I said.

"It's very beautiful," she said, shyly.

I could feel my throat begin to itch. I pushed my tongue against the top of my mouth to try to stop it, and my face screwed up in a kind of agony. I didn't even know where Lucy lived—not the town, not the circumstances. I didn't know where she worked during the day, whether or not she had family, whether or not they were in this country legally, if she was counting the dollars she could send home as she brushed and mopped and scoured. This spectacular house of glass and granite and bamboo was mine. I was the queen. This was my castle—and I was so ungrateful. I started to cry.

"Señora?" Lucy asked.

"It *is* beautiful," I said, through my tears. "Thank you."

"Why do you cry?" she asked, and put her hand on my arm. Her hand was warm and plump.

Lucy didn't know a single one of my friends. I wouldn't see her at church or at Jackie's school, at the grocery store or the gym. She would never be at one of the parties we might throw in this house—cocktails at sunset, a dinner party for eight, a celebration for Jackie's graduation. She was just a warm body, just someone standing there a few days before this house would officially be mine. "I fell in love with a house by the beach," I said. "An old house being sold by an old woman."

"Oh!" Lucy said, her face brightening, her head nodding. "The house from the paper."

I gaped. "You know about it?"

"My father," Lucy said. "He has a friend who mows the lawns on that street."

"Are you serious?"

Lucy nodded vigorously. "My whole family, we went there when you could walk around inside. We took flan."

"Your family is trying to win that house, Lucy?" I asked.

She beamed. "My five uncles. One of them owns a nursery in San Diego."

"Where do you live?" I asked.

"Gardena," she said. "Five brothers and sisters and two cousins all in one house. It's hot there in the summer. I try to study at night, you know, and it's always hot. I love to live near the beach."

"You're going to school?"

"To work for a dentist," she said.

"You'll be very good at that," I said.

When I got back in the car after leaving the houseplants, I called Vanessa.

"So you're not mad at me?" she asked.

"I'm completely pissed at you," I said.

"I figured."

"But can I ask you something about the house by the beach?"

"No, ma'am," she said. "I'm staying out of that one. I'm staying a mile away."

"I just want to know how many people have made bids for it. I mean, is it hundreds? Thousands?"

"I personally know seven people trying to get that house," Vanessa said, "not including you, since I don't really know where you stand. And between the rest of the agents in the office, I know of several dozen more. And every other agency in town is the same. I heard the *Today* show is going to do the story," she said.

"What is it about that house?"

"You mean besides the chance to walk away with a two-million-dollar property for three hundred thousand?"

"Besides that."

"It's a house that's lasted a long time in a world where nothing much lasts anymore," Vanessa said.

"You've been there, haven't you?" I asked.

"April, I'm allowed to go to an open house, for God's sake."

"I'm sorry," I said. "Do you think I'm crazy to try to get it?"

"I'm a real estate agent," Vanessa said, "and your best friend. Crazy is par for the course."

"So did you learn anything that might help me? Did you learn any secrets?"

"She loves dogs," Vanessa said.

I couldn't sleep that night. I pictured Rick with a woman in a pale yellow polo shirt stretched taut across her chest, and a pale yellow skirt that rose impossibly high on her legs. Her shoes were white. Her teeth were white. She knew exactly how to apply eye makeup. And her skin. The skin of her breasts. My mind kept coming back to her skin. That, after all, was the thing you touched. It was the thing you kissed, the thing you licked. Skin was the thing that was talked about incessantly during my treatment for breast cancer—the skin they would radiate; the burns it would induce; the way skin would look without hair of any kind; the difference in the quality of the skin they would take from the stomach compared to the skin they would be replacing on the breast; the way the tape that held the gauze would make the skin raw, over time; the way a wound would fill in until it became even with the surface of the skin and then how the healing would change so that a scar would form, stretching across the skin. I tried to picture another man touching my scars, licking my tattoo, gently removing the chocolate brown bra, but all that did was make my skin crawl.

$\mathcal{M}$ONDAY

I had a ten-minute slot in which to interview Chuck Williams for my eight-hundred-word piece, after which his handlers would cut me off, but he spoke to me as if he had all day and would rather be doing nothing besides chatting with a stranger about common kitchen gadgets. "I buy what I like, and I like things that are well-designed," he said. "Things that are well made, that perform a function."

"What are some of your favorites?"

"I still like the porcelain creamer shaped like a cow,"

he said. "That was one of the first things I stocked in the original store and we're still selling them today."

"What about your kitchen at home? What do you most often use?"

"My favorite piece of kitchen equipment is a small sauté pan with a lid," he said. "I cook at home for myself and that pan is ideal for making a sauce or a stew."

I wanted to weep at the thought of this old man cooking dinner for himself in his apartment. He was head of a three-billion-dollar company and he had to make himself stew at night?

"A sauté pan?" I asked. I was just trying to buy a moment to recover.

"I appreciate things that will last a lifetime," he said. "I like things that I know will look good a hundred years from now."

I wanted to ask Chuck Williams how he could face the sauté pan every night knowing that it would probably outlive him. That pan would be used in someone else's kitchen, passed down and passed around for years after he was gone. How could he bear it?

Instead, I thanked him for his time. He had given

me more usable quotes in less time than anyone I'd ever interviewed.

~~~

After my first breast surgery, Vanessa tried to cheer me up by taking me to get my nails done. It was supposed to be a soothing afternoon activity, but I cringed through-out the entire manicure. The manicurist, with her sharp tools, felt exactly like a surgeon or a radiologist or the nurse who hooked up the chemo lines. I had to fight the whole time not to yank my hands out of hers. An energy healer was a somewhat easier indulgence because when you're naked, leaping off the table is not an option.

A woman with unexpectedly bad skin led me into a small room down a well-lit hallway. She lit a candle and asked me to change into the striped cotton gown that was folded neatly on the massage table. "Bra off, panties on," she said—and I smiled to think of all the strange places I'd heard those words.

I lay down on the table. It was covered in white cotton terry cloth that had been heated from within. Someone knocked, and the woman with bad skin came in. She took a fleece blanket, also heated, and lay it over me with the care of a mother tucking her newborn in to sleep. "Comfortable?" she asked.

"Yes, thank you," I said.

"Dr. Kim will be with you in a moment," she said. "Enjoy the music."

I closed my eyes. The sound, which filled the room from speakers wired into the ceiling, came from a flute. It sounded like a Gregorian chant played by a wood-wind. It was beautiful and eerie. I tried to pick out a pattern, but couldn't discern one. Soon there was another knock on the door and Dr. Kim walked in.

"You like the music?" he asked. "It's my favorite. Native American flute."

"Yes," I said. "I like it."

"Good!" His voice was like a gong, deep and resonant. He had shoulder-length hair that had been pulled back into a ponytail. His eyes were very narrow and black and I could feel him assessing me already, peering at me. He was a polished, handsome man—the kind that you might see on the cover of *GQ*. The comfort I had felt a few moments before as I lay near-naked under the heated blanket had vanished. He glanced at the papers I had filled out in the front room.

"You have one girl?" he asked.

"That's right."

"How old?"

"Fifteen."

"Ah!" he said, as if this were significant.

"And how long have you been married?"

"Sixteen years."

"And you are building a house, you say?"

"Yes."

"Big house?"

I laughed. "Huge," I said.

"You say here that you are agitated? This is why you are here?"

I felt tears well up in my eyes.

Dr. Kim put his hand on the top of my head. "Let me look at your tongue."

I opened my mouth.

"Stick out your tongue," he said. "Ahhhhh."

I stuck it out and he scribbled something on the

papers. He took my pulse on my left wrist, then my right and wrinkled his brow as if detecting something serious.

"OK!" he said, suddenly. "We'll start with your feet."

I nodded, as if I knew what would happen next. He peeled the blanket back to my knees and lifted my left foot. He pinched the tendons above the heel, which hurt. "Breathe," he commanded, and demonstrated by taking a deep drink of air. "Breathe until there is no pain."

I did as I was told.

After taking several breaths, the pain of his pinching was gone. He moved his fingers to one of my toes and gave me the same command. For an hour, all I did was lie in various positions and breathe into the places where, as if by magic, Dr. Kim knew I was hurting. The next thing I knew, he was telling me that it was time for me to dress. He walked out briskly and shut the door.

A few minutes later, he knocked and came back into the little room.

"You must forgive him," he said, abruptly.

"Excuse me?"

"You must forgive him," he repeated.

I just stared, incredulous. "My husband?"

He nodded.

"For what?"

"The color inside your head is very red. The color of rage. It's too hot. He loves you?"

"My husband?" I asked again, and then because I knew that he was the person in question and I knew without a doubt what the answer was, I said, "Yes."

"Maybe you must forgive him for loving you. Twenty minutes, morning and night," he said, exactly as if he were giving me instructions for gargling with salt water or soaking my feet. He put his hand on the doorknob. "And when you are done with this twenty minutes," he added, "then you forgive yourself."

I managed to speak in time to stop him from disappearing. "For what?" I asked.

"Not allowing it."

I got in the car and drove the four blocks to Pepper Tree Lane. As I drove by, I saw Peg Torrey standing in her front yard. There were two dogs lying at her feet—big black Labradors. Peg was picking lemons from a tree that looked like it could be in a painting. There were dozens of huge, very yellow lemons hanging amid glossy green leaves. She was placing them one by one in a basket. I parked at the end of the street and walked back, as if I were a regular walking the neighborhood or someone who was coming back from a stroll on the beach. I stopped at the end of her walkway, bracing myself for the dogs to leap up. They lifted their heads, hauled themselves up and padded softly over to sniff my shoes. The dogs were old.

"It's a great day for lemonade," I said.

Peg smiled. "I was thinking of lemon meringue pie." I noticed that she was not wearing the necklace I'd left on the doorknob yesterday. The only jewelry she had on was her wedding ring.

"With a tree like that, you could have lemons for breakfast, lunch and dinner."

She laughed. "This tree has been producing fruit like this for thirty years, every season of the year. My daughter used to say it was magic."

"What's your secret?" I asked. One of the dogs continued to sniff at one of my feet. The other dog lay down next to my other foot, pinning me to where I stood.

Peg dropped a lemon in her basket. "We planted it over the ashes of a very special dog," she said.

"I'm sorry," I said.

Peg laughed again, a full throated guffaw. "No need to apologize," she said, "it was a long time ago. Her name was Little Ann."

I may not be a dog lover, but I was one of those kids who stayed up late reading books under the covers when I was supposed to be asleep. I burned out a lot of flashlights in my day. "Like Little Ann from *Where the Red Fern Grows*?" I asked.

Peg held the lemon in her hand and turned her body toward me. "Yes," she said, and then she seemed to notice that her dogs were in my personal space. "Pete," she called. "Pretzel." She whistled softly and the dogs returned to their spot on the grass in the shade of the lemon tree.

"She wasn't a coon dog, was she?"

"Cocker spaniel," Peg said.

"My daughter wants a dog for Christmas," I said, "and she's always wanted one of those." I was very careful with my words. I felt like it was important not to lie. "Would you recommend one?"

"We've always had retrievers since Little Ann," Peg said, "and I actually never knew her. She was my husband's dog before I met him."

I nodded, as if this explained the magic of the tree. I was about to continue walking. I felt as if I had stayed long enough and felt satisfied by having heard this story about the dog and the tree and thirty years of lemons. When I glanced up to wave good-bye, however, I noticed that there were tears running down Peg's cheeks. She was just standing there in her front yard, crying. She saw me see her, and she smiled.

"It's such an old story," she said, and waved her hand as if to dismiss it.

I stood stock-still and prayed for her to keep talking.

"I killed Little Ann," she said. "It's how I met Harry. I hit her with my car."

I pictured a rainy night. A young woman driving a car with a stick shift. A sickening thud. A man crouched at the dog's head, cradling the animal in his arms. The dog howling into the rainy night. The young woman leaping from her car, screaming. And something happening in the next few moments that led to an introduction, dinner perhaps, then almost fifty years of marriage.

"I used to picture her in heaven," Peg said. "Dog heaven, where God takes you for a walk every day and the angels feed you bones. But now that Harry's gone, I'm not sure heaven works like that. I just can't be at all sure."

"It's a nice thought, though," I said.

The front door opened and Peg's daughter came out onto the front porch.

"The crust is ready, Mom," she said. "It's time for you to come in." She glared at me, taking my measure and determining, correctly, that I was just another in the parade of suitors who were trying to get the house. I wanted to call out that I'd done nothing to persuade her mother. I'd left nothing, said nothing, done nothing that could be construed as a manipulative bid. I hadn't even told Peg Torrey my name.

Peg called her dogs, picked up her basket of lemons,

nodded at me, and went inside. I turned to walk back down the street—and ran straight into the woman with the poodles. She was wielding a small statuette in her hand like a weapon.

"What Peg needs is this statue of Saint Joseph to smooth the sale of that house," the woman said. "You want to put your Saint Joseph right at the base of the sign, head down, facing the house."

While we were talking, a woman drove up in a mini-van and parked. She opened the back door and lifted out a little lemon tree in a terra-cotta vase. It appeared to be quite heavy. She struggled to make her way up the walkway and left the tree on the front steps. There was a small white envelope poking through the branches like a flag.

"You see?" the woman with the poodles said, as if the gift of a tree were evidence of the power of Saint Joseph.

I excused myself and walked back to the car. While I was pulling away from the curb, I saw a white pickup truck pulling up to the house across the street from the bungalow. The bed was crammed with brooms and rakes, lawnmowers and leaf blowers. I drove by and peered into the driver's side window. There was a brown-skinned man putting on a straw hat. I looked at his face, craning my neck to see if he had Lucy's nose or her smile, and wondering where he lived, what his home was like and whether or not he was happy.

When I got in the car, I sat in the warm silence and tried to do what the energy healer had suggested.

"I forgive him," I said out loud, "for loving me."

The thing I thought about in response was a trip we took to Yellowstone National Park before Jackie was born. I had gone there as a child and remembered being marched into the Old Faithful Inn and made to stare up at the balconies that looked like a wooden layer cake, and to sit on the verandah and watch the geyser go off. But my parents were look-and-run vacationers; they never stopped and stayed, and I'd always wanted to stay in that grand old hotel. Rick planned the whole trip—rooms, reservations in the dining room, the whole deal.

When we got to the hotel, he led me through the lobby, running his hands along the wood railings, tracing all the angles and curves, explaining the beauty of mortise-and-tenon joinery. We sat in front of the enormous stone fireplace, drinking hot chocolate and staring up at the exposed rafters. The next day, we hiked past what must have been a hundred geysers and hot pots. We said each of their names out loud, read about the minerals that made them bloom orange and blue and waited patiently for each of them to erupt, if erupting was what they did. Once, a buffalo lumbered within a dozen feet of us, completely oblivious to our existence. It was a strange and beautiful place.

On the second night, Rick laid in wait for one of the card tables on the second floor of the inn—the ones with a view of Old Faithful itself. When one became vacant, he pounced on it, produced a deck of cards, and announced that this was where we would stay all evening. We played Go Fish and Crazy Eights until a group of people asked us when we expected to leave and Rick invited them for a game of Thirty-One. We played so late into the night that I finally went back to the room. At midnight, I poked my head out the door of our room to see him reading by the green mica lamp at one of the writing desks.

"I just love the lamp," he confessed.

On the way home, in Jackson Hole, Rick bought a piece of raw birch from a man who was selling beautiful carved salad bowls from a cart near the town square. He told me he was going to carve me a bowl. It took him three years, several power tools and many cuts on his hands, but he finally presented me with a birch salad bowl, glistening with mineral oil. It was smooth and deceptively light, about an inch thick with whorls and knots dancing across the surface. I never use that bowl for lettuce. I keep it on a shelf in the living room, testimony to Rick's calmness, patience and love.

It was common knowledge around the rental apartment building that if you were trying to get rid of a piece of furniture, all you had to do was put it on the sidewalk that led from the parking lot to the pool, and it would be gone by morning. I'd seen metal filing cabinets with dents in the side get swiped away, and old-fashioned coffee tables with elaborately turned legs. There was one upholstered chair that sat forlornly for forty-eight hours—a gold and brown thing that looked like something Archie Bunker might have owned—but on the second morning, it disappeared. We hauled our Santa Fe plaid couch down there on Monday night. It was heavy and old. Rick and I maneuvered it out the door, down the hallway, into the elevator and onto the sidewalk. It was hard work. Jackie drew a Free sign, and pinned it on the back.

As we hauled boxes of clothes and pots and toiletries down that same hallway and elevator, I must have passed that couch three dozen times. I couldn't imagine that I had ever picked it out, brought it home, slept on it, made love on it. It was like it never belonged to me, and yet there it was, waiting for new life.

"What are we going to do if no one takes the couch?" I asked Rick. We were wrapping dishes in newspaper.

"Leave it," he said.

"We can't just leave it. We'll have to haul it away."

"We're not hauling it away," he said. "Someone will take it."

⁓

When I walked down to the parking lot the next morning on my way to the new house, the couch was gone. I stood there and stared at the place where it had been, wondering if it had ever really existed.

$\mathcal{T}$UESDAY

Whenever a new magazine is launched, the new editors invariably say that they're going to produce stories that speak to real women about the things that really matter to them—and then they come out with an issue that looks like every other women's magazine you've ever seen. There are only so many magazine stories. There are the you-can-do-anything-with-your-life stories, the how-to-please-your-man stories and the seasonal stories that appear like clockwork: spring cleaning, Christmas shopping, back to school, moving. The strange reality of life for people who work on these magazines is that you're always working on these stories at least six months ahead, so in summer, you're writing Valentine's Day pieces, and on Valentine's Day you're working on back-to-school articles. Moving tips are usually featured in the summer, which means that someone was working on them in the dead cold of winter when no one in their right mind would move unless they happen to live in Southern California.

What they recommend is that you meticulously label your boxes with a system of rooms and numbers and colors and that you make a master list of what's inside. You would have stickers. You would feel in control. But does anyone really do that? We had boxes marked "Garage + laundry detergent" and "toaster, blender, bath mat + printer ink." In a box with Rick's mother's wedding china, I'd stuck some elastic exercise bands. On top of sheets, I'd placed cans of refried beans we had yet to eat. I told the movers to put the boxes wherever they wanted.

When the piano guys came, I directed them to the spot in the living room where the piano had been drawn on the blueprint the very first time I saw it. They hauled it in, and then started to remove the bubble wrap, which had been repaired with duct tape where I had slashed it the other day.

"No, don't," I said abruptly to a man wearing a John Deere baseball cap.

"Don't what?"

"Don't unwrap it," I said.

"Can't set it up if we don't unwrap it," he said.

"I know," I said. "That's OK. I'm not sure where I want it, is all. I'll have to call and have you come back when I'm ready."

"That'll be an extra charge," he said.

I nodded. "I know."

After the piano guys were gone, Rick bounced in from the garage and said, "Time to get a Christmas tree!"

I wanted to make up the beds, get food in the fridge, find my toothbrush and try to stake a claim, but I knew I couldn't protest. It was two days before Christmas, and we needed a tree.

We piled in Rick's truck and headed to Home Depot. They always had a Christmas lot with trees hauled in daily from Oregon. They blocked off an area with a chain-link fence, set up two guys with chain saws to trim the trunks, and piped in Christmas carols while people lined up to pick out their Douglas firs. Despite the black-top and the curbs and the white slash of painted lines, it always smelled like a pine forest. You would think the scene would be a sad example of crass commercialism, but I always liked it. There was something miraculous about being able to pick out a fir tree from Oregon right there in a Southern California parking lot, making sure that the branches were exactly as far apart as you wanted them to be and that the top tapered just so. There was something picturesque about tying it with twine to the roof of your car no matter where you were.

When we pulled up to Home Depot, however, there were no chain-link fences, no chain saws, no lines of festive families picking out their trees. There was one hand-painted sign on a lamppost: XMAS TREES SOLD OUT!

"Let's go to that lot over on Hawthorne," Jackie suggested, "the one where they always have that creepy pumpkin patch."

"They charge eighty-five dollars for a five-foot tree," Rick said. "It's a total rip-off."

"But we need a tree," I said.

We drove over to Hawthorne and could immediately tell that there were no trees at that lot, either. Bales of hay lay under the strings of white and red lights, but there were no crowds of people, no forest of trees. A few green branches were scattered across the parking lot. Wired to the fence was a sign that read SOLD OUT.

A feeling of panic began to set in. Christmas without a tree? Our first Christmas in a new house and no tree? "Target!" I said suddenly. "The Crenshaws said they got their tree at Target."

We drove to the sprawling store, parked and made our way through the Christmas decoration displays to the garden center. There was no one there, but propped up against the wooden guardrails that had been constructed for just this purpose were a handful of evergreens. Jackie dashed to the nearest one and hauled it up. It came up to her nose and was fat, like a gumdrop. She let it fall back against the rails.

Rick hefted another upright. "How does it look?" he asked. It had a gaping hole on one side and a crooked top.

"It looks like Charlie Brown's tree," Jackie said.

We evaluated all the trees that were there—six of them—and decided the Charlie Brown tree was the best. It took us half an hour to get someone to come out and ring us up, and then there was no string to tie it down. We threw it into the back of Rick's truck, but before he even started the ignition, Jackie said, "Mom? Where are all the decorations?"

I thought of the boxes scattered throughout the house, in bedrooms and closets, in the garage and the dining room. Somewhere in that forest of cardboard were six boxes of Christmas decorations that we'd been collecting ever since Jackie was a child. There were delicate glass teardrops, a little mouse on a ladder stringing lights, marshmallow snowmen, a Santa on skis and paper snowflakes Jackie had made out of magazines when she was three. I knew they were somewhere in the house, but I had no idea where to even begin to look.

We went back into Target and bought three boxes of cheap red balls. On sale. $3.99 each.

We had a party to go to that night—an open house at the home of one of Rick's biggest clients. I wore my black pants, the red sweater, the gold earrings, and a pasted-on smile. I didn't feel like having eggnog or mulled cider. I tried a piece of homemade shortbread, but it was so dry and bland that I turned my back, spit it into my green napkin and threw it in the trash. Rick laughed and drank, and wanted to stay late, but we had left Jackie home alone in a brand-new house with a bunch of cardboard boxes. The TV wasn't plugged in. Stuff was piled on all the chairs and couches. I kept picturing her sitting there freaking out, feeling the dark of the night pressing in on her. Rick finally agreed to leave around 9:00. On the way home, I put both my hands on the steering wheel and carefully navigated the hill back to our house.

We found Jackie sitting on a bar stool at the big central island in the kitchen. Music was blaring from the computer, which she had set up on the counter, and a little mound of M&M's was piled up beside it. She had filled a jar with M&M's and wrapped it with red tissue paper. "Hi, Mom, hi, Dad," she said.

"What are you doing?" I asked.

"Burning a CD for Max for Christmas," she said. "He's taking off to go skiing tomorrow."

"When did you get this stuff?"

"Yesterday with Tania," she said.

I nodded, then suddenly remembered that I hadn't gotten a gift for Vanessa.

"Can I use some of the paper?" I asked.

"Knock yourself out," she said. "I'm going to sleep." She flicked off her computer and hopped off the stool.

"Do you need anything?" I asked.

"Just to go to sleep," she said. "I'm fine."

I kissed her and watched her go up the stairs to her big bedroom with the big window seat and the big walk-in closet.

I fished my little Buddha out of my purse, wrapped it in red tissue paper and dropped it into the bag with the pumpkin-colored spatula. On one of the cards left over from Jackie's soldier project, I wrote:

This is the Buddha of Long Life, but I think he'll work as the Buddha of Long Friendship, too. Thank you for being there for me so often.
xxoo, April

When I got up to the bedroom, Rick was sound asleep.

I found my toothbrush and a washcloth and stepped into the magnificent bathroom. The Swiss Coffee on the walls gleamed like polished pearls. Lucy had scrubbed the new tile and left the mirrors dust- and streak-free. There was so much room in that bathroom, I could have danced, if I'd felt like it. I took off my party clothes and stepped into the shower. There was a huge overhead faucet with multiple settings—for every hour of the day, it seemed. I dialed to one that would pummel me with hot water, then blasted the water, hung my head and cried.

CHRISTMAS EVE

On Christmas Eve day I sat at the kitchen counter and wrote about Chuck Williams and his love of the white porcelain cow creamer, of a little sauté pan and of things that would last a lifetime. He had more faith in that pan than I did in my whole house.

When it was time to get ready for dinner, I went upstairs, walked into the bedroom and saw Peg Torrey on television. Rick was sitting on the edge of the bed, a shoe in his hand. Our TV was sitting on a box by the window and on the TV, Peg Torrey was sitting in the front room of her house—it was all wood and sunlight. She was wearing khaki pants and a crisp white shirt I felt certain her daughter had ironed. She was sitting on the leather couch next to a reporter who was wearing a tweed pencil skit and a jacket with a cinched waist.

"We're back with Peg Torrey, the Southern California widow whose offer to sell her house at below market value to the buyer who can prove he's worthy has sparked a real estate frenzy this holiday season.

"Is it true that you were offered three million cash and turned it down?"

"That's right," she said.

"You weren't even tempted?"

"I'm seventy-eight years old," she said. "I don't need three million dollars."

"Can you tell us about some of the other things people have sent to try to win your favor?"

"There's been a lot of chocolate and a lot of wine, a painting of the house."

"And have any of these things caught your eye?"

"They're all lovely," she said, "but none of them is right."

"How will you know when you find what's right?" the reporter asked. You could tell by her face and by the way she held her body that she knew she had a gem of a story.

Peg smiled. She had a beautiful smile. It lit up her whole face. "I don't know," she said, "but I'll know it when I do."

"Do you have a deadline?"

"My daughter has given me until New Year's Day," she said.

The reporter leaned in. "Why are you doing this, Mrs. Torrey? You lost your husband just a few weeks ago. It's the holidays. Why go through the hassle of having so many strangers vying for your attention?"

"It's hard for people these days to understand, but I was a housewife for forty-nine years. I was married as much to this house as I was to my husband. I can't stay here another minute without him. I can't bear it. But I won't just throw the house to the wolves. I helped my husband die, and I'll help this house in the same way. I'll usher it to a good place. For a house, a good place means people who will be alive in it, who will draw on all the years of love that happened here, and add layers of their own."

The reported turned toward the camera. "Back to you, Katie, from the last beach bungalow on Pepper Tree Lane."

When the segment was over, Rick switched off the TV and finished putting on his shoes. But he didn't say a word.

Christmas Eve in the Episcopal Church is an extravagant affair. There are the banks of outrageously bright red poinsettias, the sprays of evergreen, the flickering candles, and more people than the church was ever meant to hold. The congregants shoehorn themselves into the pews with tight-lipped smiles. Any woman who has a fur, whether real or fake, always wears it, and wool coats come out of the closet, too, so that the prevailing smell in the church is wet dog. There's always a trumpet, a soprano to sing the first lines of "Once in Royal David's City," and a full choir dressed in neatly pressed red robes. You sit there waiting for something to happen. And there is always the feeling that something *is* going to happen. It's an occasion, after all, an event—the thing you've been working toward for weeks.

What I thought about, for the most part, was my mother. She was in Chicago. My brother, his wife and kids would have had her over to their house for a very elaborate meal served on very elaborate china and silver. The conversation would have been wholly about the food—the unusual choice of fennel for the stuffing, the surprising richness of the pea soup. At church, they would all sit in the same pew they always sat in and my mother would sing the hymns in a voice that sounded as if it were coming from her nose. People would stare, because she sang so loudly and sounded so strange, and because when it came time to sing "Silent Night," she would start to cry, and her voice would crack, and she would be overcome, but she wouldn't stop singing. It had always been so, and it was a memory that made me cry, when we sang our version of "Silent Night" in our coastal town of California, because singing "Silent Night" on

Christmas Eve was the only time I could ever remember my mother expressing much feeling for anything at all.

I also thought about Rick's mother and father and how nice it would have been if they'd still been with us. I liked them. I liked being part of their family.

If someone had asked me what the sermon was about that Christmas Eve, I would have had to say that I had absolutely no idea.

We got home from church at midnight and all three of us went straight to sleep. I thought I heard something around 2:00, but figured it was just the unfamiliar noises of a new house. At 3:30, I awoke and couldn't sleep. I was hot, I was hungry. I tossed and turned until 4:00, then finally got out of bed and went downstairs for a glass of milk. When I moved toward the refrigerator I accidentally stepped into a brown paper shopping bag and spilled garbage all over the pristine bamboo floors. I turned on a dim light, reached down to gather up the

Subway wrappers and soda cans from our moving day lunch, and noticed Rick's handwriting on the lined paper from one of Jackie's school notebooks. I uncrumpled it and read what he had written:

Dear Mrs. Torrey,
My name is Rick Newton. I'm a custom home builder here in the South Bay. My wife is a writer. We have a daughter who's a junior at South High. We're currently building a home on Vista del Mar.

There were wads of paper everywhere. I sat on the floor to read them one by one:

Dear Mrs. Torrey,
I've lived in Redondo Beach my entire life. There's nowhere else I'd rather live.

Dear Mrs. Torrey,
I've built houses all my life and I've always believed in good craftsmanship.

Dear Mrs. Torrey,

I've worked with my hands all my life, so putting words on paper isn't easy for me.

Dear Mrs. Torrey,

I met my wife when I was 29 years old, but I feel like I've known her forever, and I need your house to make sure I do.

Dear Mrs. Torrey,

Houses are tricky things.

Dear Mrs. Torrey,

If anyone asked me why I love my wife so much I'd never be able to explain it. The same is true about your house.

Dear Mrs. Torrey,

Fuck you.

I smoothed out the notes, then went to Jackie's backpack and ripped out two pieces of paper from her binder. She had one of those tiny staplers in her pencil case. I used that to turn one of the pieces of paper into a makeshift envelope. I used an erasable pen and wrote my own letter:

Dear Mrs. Torrey,

My husband doesn't know I'm sending these letters. I found them crumpled up on the floor just now, very early on Christmas Day. We used to make a big deal out of setting things up so that our little girl would believe Santa had come. We would eat the cookies she left out, drink the milk, fill her stocking with chocolate. We wanted her to believe in Santa because it seemed so close to believing in God, and believing in God seemed really important to us. You have to believe in something, right?

That little girl is 15 now and I don't think she believes much in either Santa Claus or God. I didn't think I did, either, until just now. Seeing these letters from Rick scattered on this floor was the closest I've come to believing in a long time, because it's the closest I've come to being known for who I am. It felt exactly like a moment of grace. And it made me realize that this might be what you're looking for, as well.

You're just looking for a moment of grace, a moment when your house and all the years you've lived in it are seen for exactly what they are. I wish I could give you that moment of grace wrapped up in a bow this Christmas morning because even though you don't know me from any one of the thousands of people who've traipsed through your life these past few weeks, you've given it to me.

Merry Christmas,

April Newton

I slipped back into bed somewhere close to 5:00. It was still dark. Then, around 6:00, I heard Rick start to stir. He turned over, shifted his weight so that he was lying on his back. I was on my side, turned away from him, as had become my habit. Normally, I would have slipped out of bed. Normally, I would have pretended that I didn't hear the way his breath had changed from a sleeping breath to a waking breath.

I rolled over and pressed a leg against Rick's body.

He reached his arm over and rested it against the thick part of my hips.

I was astonished at how warm his skin felt.

I moved closer so that my stomach pressed against his hip and my breasts pressed against his chest.

He began to rub his thumb over my hip bone, very slowly.

"I love you," I whispered.

He shifted his weight so that he was facing me and gently kissed my lips. I pressed my body more firmly into his and opened my mouth to kiss him back. I moved so that I could welcome him.

Then the phone rang.

We heard Jackie answering down the hallway, then her footsteps coming toward our room. I turned away, pulled the sheets up to my chin.

She knocked.

"It's Grandma," she said, handing me the phone. My mom. Calling from Chicago where she would be ruling a kitchen that wasn't hers and whipping up animosity from my brother's wife as surely as she was whipping up the mashed potatoes.

"Merry Christmas," she said with cool efficiency. I was an item that needed to be checked off her list. It was a long list that included braising and broiling, separating and grilling.

"Merry Christmas, Mom," I said.

"How's the house?"

"I don't really know yet," I said.

"I bet you'll be happy to finally cook in a real kitchen."

"Yes," I said. "How's Cal?"

"Fine," she said. "We're all fine."

The call went on for fifteen minutes, even though we had nothing to say. When I finally hung up, Rick had slipped on his sweatpants and gone downstairs with Jackie to start making pancakes.

CHRISTMAS DAY

We sat on the floor around the sad Target Christmas tree. I gave Rick the laser tape measure, which I knew he liked because he immediately got out the instructions and started to read about how the thing worked. We made Jackie close her eyes as we walked her to the den, where we had laid out all the new things for her room—the beanbag chair and the desk, the fluffy rug and an alarm clock in the shape of a beagle. She flung herself onto the beanbag and asked if she could open her present from Max.

It was in the pocket of her robe—a tiny box with something written right onto the cardboard with ball-point pen. She read the words, pulled off the top and gasped. It was a yin/yang necklace on a leather string. She slipped it over her head, gushing, "Isn't it so amazing?"

It was so amazing, in fact, that I felt choked up. "That's very sweet," I managed to say.

There was a large box under the Christmas tree from my mother. Jackie handed me the card that said, "For your new bedroom." Rick and I had imagined our new bedroom as a clean, neutral space, earthy and plain like the beach. It would be our retreat from the loud and noisy world, our perch overlooking the ocean. The ceiling beams were sandblasted and whitewashed. The rug was the color of sand. The comforter I had selected was the palest shade of turquoise blue, my ultimate response to the Swiss Coffee on the walls.

Inside my mother's box was a complete set of linens for our new bedroom—a heavy Ralph Lauren pattern in red and blue paisley, with a white eyelet dust ruffle, blue pillow shams, a red throw pillow, and a matching set of towel sheets, bath mat, hand towels and washcloths. It looked like the bedroom set of a hunting lodge.

"Oh, dear," I said.

"Mom, it's Christmas," Jackie warned me. "Be nice."

I bit my lip, and then Rick pulled a box out from under the tree. It was a large, flat rectangle wrapped in plain brown paper.

"The gals at the planning commission dug it up for me," Rick said.

I tore open the paper, expecting a photo of the newly finished house, or the blueprints framed for posterity. It was an aerial photo of Redondo Beach taken a very long time ago. You could see the pier and the curve of the Esplanade, but there were few trees, few roads and few houses. It looked like something familiar, yet foreign at the same time. I couldn't figure it out.

I looked up at Rick. "What is it?"

"It was taken the year the house was built," he said. "I thought she might like it."

The gears in my mind were grinding, but I still didn't understand. "Who?" I asked.

"Peg Torrey," he said.

"Who's she?" Jackie asked.

"You sound like you practically know her," I said to Rick.

"I've been inside the house."

"You have? When?"

"While you were having your massage."

"But I . . ."

"Vanessa took me through. She is, after all, a Realtor."

"What is it, Mom?" Jackie asked, positioning herself behind me so she could see the photo. "And who is Peg Torrey?"

"She's a woman who owns a bungalow down by the beach."

"Why did Dad give you a picture of someone else's house?"

"Because it's exactly what I wanted."

"An old photo?"

I shook my head. "The chance to follow a whim."

Jackie stood up. She wasn't fooled for a minute. "What kind of a whim?" she asked.

The problem with setting a precedent for telling the

truth to your children is that you have to keep it up. You can't suddenly decide that you're going to start lying, or that you're going to pick and choose. They understand what truth is, and once you give it to them, they expect it. All the time. There was never a moment when I was going to lie to Jackie about having cancer. She was only ten, and I may have used softer words, or softer concepts, but I told her the truth. I met a woman a few years ago who was a fifteen-year cancer survivor. Her children were grown, with children of their own, and houses far away. "I'm still wondering," she told me, "how I'm going to tell my children I had cancer." I was speechless. I had no advice for her whatsoever. She was too late for the truth.

"Peg Torrey is giving her house away in a contest," I explained, "and I thought I'd try to enter."

Jackie squinted at me. She stood up even straighter so that she looked like some kind of angry queen. She looked at her dad, then back at me, and at the photo in my hands.

"You're kidding," she said, flatly.

"It's hard to explain," I said.

"Dad built this house for you," she said. "That's like...it's like. I swear, it's like having an affair."

"Jackie!"

She spun on her heels, grabbed her purse and walked past the Christmas tree and all the presents and out the door.

I got up to follow her.

"Don't," Rick said. He'd stepped in front of me, pressed his hand against my arm.

"Don't what?"

"Don't go after her."

"It's Christmas! We don't even know where she's going!"

"Probably just down the hill. I'll go after her. Why don't you take that photo over to Peg Torrey's house."

"Rick, that's crazy. Let me go." He was still holding on to my arm.

"Didn't you listen to the sermon last night?"

"The sermon? Please. Let me go."

"It was about how we tell the same story year after year and say the same prayers and sing the same songs, but we never know where the magic is going to come on any given year. We never know when we're going to feel moved. All the anticipation—the gifts and the decorating—it's all just about waiting, and watching for when we're going to feel moved."

"What does that have to do with anything?"

"You might find what you're looking for if you take that photo over today."

"I just want to find Jackie."

"I said I would go."

I don't know what shifted—the planets in their courses, the molecules in the air, the way the blood flowed through my head—but I let him win. I let Jackie go. I allowed myself to honor the gift he'd given me.

"OK," I said.

I took the photo and gathered up the letters we'd written to Peg Torrey and drove down the hill to Pepper Tree Lane. The daughter I had met at the open house was sitting on the front steps drinking a cup of coffee. She looked tired. There was a large basket tied up with cellophane sitting next to her, and a bottle of merlot with a plaid bow.

"It's like gifts from the Magi," I said.

She laughed. "That's good," she said.

"Shall I just add my offerings to the pile, then?"

"Go right ahead."

I set down the gift-wrapped photo and the homemade envelope of letters, but felt like I should say something before turning to leave. "It's a lovely house," I said.

I wrote an article for *Family Circle* last year on the ten rules for good conversation. It was supposed to be a primer for mothers who were having trouble talking to their daughters, or wives having trouble talking to their spouses. My expert source was a young professor from Cornell who had done a study that involved timing people's responses in conversation. Step number one for good communication, she said, was to allow the empty spaces in the conversation time to expand. You were supposed to breathe in and breathe out two whole cycles before talking again after you asked a question, which was the equivalent of twenty seconds. I breathed, and breathed again, and just like that, Sarah started talking.

"I know," she said. "Most of the houses on the street were like this when I was little. There was a Foster's

Freeze a few blocks that way on Pacific Coast Highway and all the kids would go over there for chocolate-dipped ice cream cones. And there was a restaurant the other way called Millie Riera's. It was right on the water. I mean, you could sit there, have swordfish steaks and look out at the dolphins playing in the waves. That was the place my dad always took us for big birthdays."

"No wonder your mom wants to preserve it."

"She wants to handle the sale of the house the same way my dad would have handled the death of a patient—by being present for it, by being attentive to it, by not running away from it, by trying to find meaning in it." She stood up abruptly, then. I was standing on the sidewalk at the bottom of the front steps and she was standing on the porch. She towered above me. "It's hard to be the child of saints," she said.

She bent down and picked up the basket, the bottle of wine, my photo and my letters, then disappeared inside the front door. I imagined that the long dining room table was groaning with gifts. There were probably honey-baked hams and tins of English toffee, exotic coffee and potted poinsettias. My wish was that my offering would stand out like the house itself—that Peg Torrey would see it, and respond to it, just like I had when I came across her house on a day when I was least expecting it.

⁓

When I got home, Jackie was sitting at the kitchen counter, looking grim. I resisted the urge to hug her the way you'd hug a small child who had packed a suitcase and tried to run away.

"Dad drove me by the house," she said. She slipped off her stool and began walking toward her room. "And just so you know, I'm never living there. Never."

⁓

Vanessa had us over for Christmas dinner. She had a huge family with sisters and brothers and cousins who all lived nearby, so their holidays were always loud and boisterous. They often roasted three turkeys, and people brought everything from Jell-O salads to nutmeg martinis. Jackie disappeared into the rec room with Tom and the other kids. I spent much of the evening talking to Jane, a friend of one of Vanessa's sisters, who was a breast cancer survivor of ten years. She had recently opened a boutique in Hermosa Beach called p*i*n*k. It was an upscale clothing shop that sold Isabella Fiori purses for $450 a pop, and Diesel jeans for $265, and she wanted to pick my brain about publicity. What was the best way to get to the fashion editors, she asked, and how did you go about sending around a press release? I asked her what her hook was because usually when people ask me that question, they're talking about an aunt who ran in a marathon or an old roommate who was working in the Peace Corps and wondering how they could land them on the cover of *O, The Oprah Magazine.*

"I'm giving one hundred percent of the profits to a foundation that's running clinical trials for breast cancer patients with metastatic disease," she said.

"One hundred percent?" I asked, astonished. She had such a good story. In a world where giant corporations were donating one percent off the sale of a candle, or one dollar for every customer in the month of October, giving away every penny you make is a good story.

"I'm eager to help all women," she explained, "but I'm mostly eager to help myself."

I had assumed that when she had said ten years, she meant ten years and done. What she meant, however, was ten years and still sick, ten years and still fighting, ten years and still praying for a cure. Her hair, I now noticed, wasn't just cut fashionably short. It was growing in from chemo.

"It's a great story," I said. "I'd love to pitch it myself."

"You mean it?"

"Absolutely."

She shrugged. "At least I'm going to die surrounded by great clothes," she said.

It's possible to try to argue someone out of a stance like that—to try to say, *Oh, no, you're going to be fine* or *Come, now, you can't think like that.* But people die the way they live. To try to take that away from them or talk them out of it is to deny the power of death. There was no way I was going to do that. I laughed and told her she sure would.

Secretly, I was jealous of every single thing about that woman except for one.

It was Christmas, and she was going to die.

FRIDAY

Jackie played in the Holiday Classic, just like she promised she would. I sat in the stands, as always, and mostly watched Max watching Jackie.

"How's the boy?" Gina asked, following my line of sight.

"He's nice," I said, "but it's hard not to wonder what's going on."

"Don't you read Jackie's e-mail?"

I turned and stared. "You do that?"

"Of course I do," Gina said. "I'm the mother. It's my right."

"If Jackie found out I was reading her e-mail she'd never speak to me again."

"You can't be scared of your own daughter."

I turned back toward the game. She had a good point.

~

Jackie had thousands of e-mails, none of them with any recognizable names attached. I poked around a few threads about the Iraqi soldier project, the final paper in English, and what people were wearing to the winter formal before I stumbled on a note from Max. His screen name was flyboy247, which made some sense for a swimmer. He was having a hard time selecting a Christmas gift for her, he wrote, because he wanted to give her the whole world. He wanted her to know exactly how much he adored her, and exactly how beautiful she was, and exactly how he couldn't stand to be without her. She was, he said, the most amazing girl he'd ever known, and no mere trinket could possibly convey his feelings.

I clicked the note shut and then scanned the e-mail

list, terrified of what I would see and hungry for it at the same time.

In one note, he was supposed to be studying but was instead dreaming about holding her close.

In another, he was supposed to be doing math but instead remembering their kiss by the cafeteria.

She wrote back saying she couldn't stop thinking about it, either.

I love you, he said.

I love you, too, she said.

I clicked off and called Vanessa.

"Have you ever read Tom's e-mails?" I asked.

"All the time," she said.

"I just read through a month of Jackie's and I'm freaking out."

"What's going on?"

"She loves this boy. He loves her. I think they're going to elope."

"You don't remember being in love at that age?"

What I remembered was being in love when I was ten. There was a boy who lived next door named Charles Gray. He had a tree house in his backyard, which made him something of a rugged hero in my mind. It was built around the massive trunk of a pine tree. A big flat floor had been built around the tree trunk, with a ladder that went up through a hole right in the middle. You could see three of the neighbors' houses from the platform and a corner of the playground at school. We kept books up there in a wooden box. There was a copy of *Treasure Island* and *Stuart Little*. The paper was flaky and spotted with mold, but reading those books wasn't the point. They were the leaping-off point for adventures where we would pretend we were stranded or being chased or hiding out. When Charles was in the tree house, he would throw pinecones into my backyard. There was a thin space in the enormous hedge that separated my yard from his. I would slip through the brush and climb up the ladder. By the time I emerged on the platform, I would have assumed a persona, and our story would be set in motion.

Charles Gray was the boy I always thought I would marry. Even when we moved away and I lost touch with him, I would still dream about him and how we would meet someday on a bus or a train or a boat or a plane. But he was almost wholly the stuff of dreams. I don't recall that I ever touched him. I certainly never kissed him or exchanged passionate promises of love. And when I was fifteen and would have wanted to, I was a new kid in a new school, too shy to even say hello to the boys I liked.

"It just seems more intense than I remember," I said to Vanessa.

"Fifteen is intense," she said, "but I can promise you they're not going to elope."

"They could have sex. They could be having sex right now. They could have had sex every day for the last three weeks. Do you have any idea how many opportunities there are to have sex?"

"Jackie's not stupid," Vanessa said.

"You don't think?"

"No, I don't. But since we're talking about sex," Vanessa said, "how are things between you and Rick?"

"That's totally off topic."

"It's totally on topic and you know it."

"I'm not answering."

"You just did, and you want to know what I think?"

"Not really," I said.

"That you're worrying about the wrong people having sex."

$\mathcal{M}$ONDAY

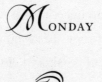

People who work in offices are always asking me how I manage to ignore the myriad distractions of working at home. There is an assumption that you need an austere cubicle in order to get anything done—that a house with piles of dishes and laundry and mail poses an overwhelming temptation. That assumption is a myth. If I'm on deadline for an assignment, I can ignore almost everything. If I've set aside a day to research stories or write pitches or do invoices, that's what I do. The only exception to that truth is when I become obsessed with something that can be looked up on the Internet. Jackie's e-mails were one of those things, but there were a finite number of them; I couldn't generate more of that story than was already there. When I ran out of material that would let me learn more about Jackie and her boyfriend, I turned, instead, to material that would tell me something about Mrs. Torrey's beach bungalow.

I looked up the original deed of sale. I looked up the property taxes. I hit upon looking up Harry Torrey and found a nearly endless stream of information. He had been a pediatric oncologist at a clinic that was part of the UCLA Medical Center. Day after day, he helped children live and he helped them die, and when he wasn't doing that, he wrote about it. I found his journal articles, op-ed pieces, excerpts he'd written for textbooks and reviews he'd written of colleagues' work. There were profiles of him in the Medical Center newsletter, tributes to him that colleagues and patients had written after he died, and announcements of gifts he and Peg had given to the hospital. He seemed like an extraordinary man.

In the course of my poking around, I learned that the

daughter, Sarah, was a baker of some renown. She was a graduate of the Culinary Institute of the Arts. She had a shop in Berkeley that was featured in a *San Jose Mercury News* series about artisan bakeries—a 1,200 word piece with a sidebar entitled "One Baker's Beginnings":

We lived half a block from the beach but I never learned to hang ten, never fell for a beach volleyball player, never really felt the golden pull of the sun. I felt drawn to our kitchen instead—a kind of blasphemy in an L.A. beach town, but our house had a great kitchen. There was a big white farm sink set on the diagonal facing the ocean. Two windows met at that corner, with no wall between them, so you could stand at the sink, and look out at the ocean, all the way up to Point Mugu—a vast expanse of blue and white chop, birds and sky. Because of the cliffs that ringed our part of the bay, you couldn't see any sand, surfers, skaters or runners from our kitchen; all that activity was hidden by the cliffs, contained down on the sand. Up above, it was just the water and sky, and the endless view.

At first, my specialty was scrambled eggs, but I soon graduated to macaroni and cheese—the real kind— which I always baked in Mom's best casserole pan, the white enameled Le Creuset with the handles. The cheese seemed to bubble best in the pan and cleanup was always a cinch. I also liked to bake cookies, but plain old oatmeal or peanut butter didn't satisfy my creative urge. Sugar cookies were my passion, and for several years in junior high, I spent whole Saturdays doing nothing but testing what temperature and time produced the perfect sugar cookie: crisp on the outside, slightly chewy on the inside and evenly golden brown. When I mastered the cookie itself, I bought a special cookie cutter at Cook N' Stuff on Palos Verdes Drive. I saved my babysitting money and rode my bike down to look at the racks of copper cookie cutters. They were one dollar each, which made them seem like the kind of tool a real cook would use. I debated getting a heart shape and a flower shape, and rejected the Christmas trees and the gingerbread men. I finally settled on a pig because I wanted to make pink icing. Whenever any of my friends or family had a birthday that year, they got a

dozen large pig sugar cookies, perfectly frosted in pink,
with little silver candy bead eyes, laid flat in a gift box,
on pink tissue paper. They were among the most spec-
tacular gifts I have ever given.

Sidebars are one of my specialties. Give me a piece on organic cotton lingerie and I'll give you a sidebar on the amount of pesticides it takes to grow the cotton needed for a conventional pair of underwear. Give me a piece on designers and their favorite chairs and I'll give you a sidebar on how Corbusier came up with the design of his iconic lounger. You want books to read? Web sites to check? I can box off information in my sleep.

There were several sidebars to the *Town & Country* sex article. One of them was about having sex when you didn't feel like it. "Many couples claim they are too tired for sex, or they refrain from sex when other things in their life aren't going well," it said. "This is counterintuitive. Sex gives you energy. Sex brings you closer. It's exactly the thing to do to reenergize a relationship." A second sidebar was called, "Setting the Stage." It was a call to action to make your sexual space sacred by making a conscious effort to engage the senses. You could use candles, scarves draped over lamps, oils with the essence of vanilla or sandalwood, and beautiful things to adorn the body. Things like lace. Silk.

I left the magazine article on my desk, drove to the village and parked my car in front of Avisha, then sat there, working up the courage to go inside. I felt as if everyone on the street were staring at me, knowing exactly what I was about to do. Finally it seemed safer to go in than it did to stay out.

Manon was behind the low counter. "Ah!" she said, when she saw me, "How can I help you today?"

"I'd like the bra," I said, as if I had been her only customer all week and she would know exactly what I was talking about.

"Of course," she said, and then walked over and plucked it off the rack—both the bra and the panties, in the size I had tried on.

"And the dress?" she asked. I loved the dress, but the dress would make such a public statement. The dress was like a neon sign. It would blare out something about myself that I wasn't sure I wanted to say—that I loved my body, that I felt good about flaunting it, and that I was comfortable with men's eyes on it. Maybe I could do that in the privacy of my big new bedroom, but I was certain I couldn't do it anywhere I'd be likely to wear that dress.

"No, thank you," I said. "This will be fine."

Manon wrapped my things in pale pink tissue paper, sealed them with a silver sticker and tucked them into a shimmering silver bag. "Enjoy," she said, and though I expected her to wink or smirk, she had only the most lovely smile.

⁓

When Jackie got home from the post-tournament pizza party, she went straight to her room to shower. I waited fifteen minutes after the water shut off before I went to check on her. The door was slightly ajar. I tapped on it, and pushed it open at the same time. Jackie was lying on her bed, her wet hair in a towel. She jerked her head up when she heard me. She was reading the *Town & Country* sex article. I could clearly see the sidebar on "Setting the Stage;" I recognized the photo and the type. She looked at me, but with an expression that was devoid of shame or embarrassment.

"Are you and Dad getting divorced?" she asked.

At other times, this question would have made me laugh. It would have seemed like the curious musings of a hypersensitive kid who has no room in her world for shades of gray. That day, however, I didn't know how to respond.

"We're fine," I said, in a voice that even I wouldn't have believed. "Remodeling is just, you know.... They say it's one of the most stressful times in a marriage. It's been hard, but we're fine."

She nodded then, and handed the sex article to me. I took a step forward, took it from her hand and folded it in half.

"Are you and Max thinking about sex?" I asked. I just blurted it. That was the only way I knew how to say something like that. There could be no deliberation, no planning.

"Mom!" she said, and wrinkled up her nose. "I'm not an idiot. I'm not about to just throw my life away at age fifteen because I like some guy!"

I wanted to tell her that sex wasn't like that. It wasn't that dangerous. I wanted to say that it was beautiful and enriching and that it could even be something close to sacred, but I didn't trust my voice to get the message right, and mostly, I was relieved at her response, so I let it lie.

"It's just my job to ask," I said.

She rolled her eyes, then turned over, dismissing me.

TUESDAY

When we woke up the next morning, I told Rick about the conversation with Jackie—about the article, and finding her reading it, what she had asked me and what I had asked her. I was focused wholly on the sex part of the scene, how awkward it had been, how scary and funny all at the same time. But just like Vanessa had, Rick leapt right over all that.

"She asked about divorce, huh?" he said. "She didn't ask if we were having wild sex?"

I didn't laugh. "That's why I pulled out that article, actually."

Rick raised his eyebrows, inviting me to say more.

"It was a how-to article. How to make it a priority. And how to think of it as a celebration of being alive."

Rick stepped toward me.

"I'm going to work on it," I said.

He took both my hands in his. He kissed first one and then another. "Let me know if you need any help practicing."

When Jackie left for school, I snuck back to her computer. Max had mailed her the lyrics to songs about longing and lust. He had mailed her greeting cards about not being able to bear being apart. In one e-mail, he asked her to wear the blue fuzzy sweater again because it made her eyes look amazing and because it was so soft to touch. "I love you in that sweater," he wrote.

I tried to go about my day, but I couldn't remember the last time Rick had told me I looked good in anything. I kept thinking about a T-shirt he used to have—an old soft green one. He often wore it when he came back from surfing in the morning, and the sight of him walking in the door with wet hair would make me swoon.

Around 2:00, I called Avisha.

"Bonjour," Manon said.

"This is April Newton," I said. "You sold me the brown bra and panties yesterday? I'd like to buy the brown dress."

I called Rick next and asked if he would pick something up for me on the way home. I gave him the address and said, "Just ask for Manon."

I don't know what time of day Rick drove down to the Village, but I could imagine the whole thing. He would have parked his truck on the street, stood in his work boots on the sidewalk and looked back and forth from the piece of paper to the lingerie store. Gallantly, he would have stepped inside that garden of silk. He would have stood in the shadows of negligees and nightgowns, amid the whisper of lacy brassieres and thongs, and his throat would have gone dry.

"I'm here to pick up something for my wife," he would have croaked.

And Manon would have swept across the store, bringing the slip of chocolate brown and the promise that his wife was, indeed, ready for a celebration.

~

When Rick came home, I met him at the door and welcomed him home with a kiss. He didn't stop to ask me what was going on, he just dropped the bag from the lingerie store and kissed me back.

"Jackie's gone," I said, after a while. He took me by the hand, led me up the stairs and started taking off my clothes. The beautiful brown bra and panties were in the closet and the brown dress was in the silver bag in the doorway. I was wearing ratty old white cotton underwear and my gray stretched-out bra. But Rick hardly noticed. The light in that bedroom was clear, with a bluish cast from all that sky and sea. He traced his fingers on my face and on my belly and along all my scars. I just stood there, trying to feel his touch, trying to really feel it, and what I felt was electric. I remembered the *Town & Country* article and all the talk about being present and honoring each other's bodies as sacred, so wherever Rick touched me, I touched him back. Ear, ear, heart, heart. After awhile, he caught on to what I was doing and began to touch me in places that harbored even more heat. It was magic, because we were both giving and receiving all at the same time.

"I want to throw you down on this bed and ravage you," he finally said.

I smiled and whispered in his ear, "I wish you would."

It was over rather quickly. It had, after all, been a while. I lay there, suddenly, with tears running down my cheeks.

"Are you OK?" Rick asked.

"Just happy," I said.

FRIDAY

Three days later, I unfolded the *Beach Reporter* and saw
this headline:

Local Family Wins Right to Buy Beach Bungalow

The family, it turned out, had written Peg a letter from
the point of view of their dog. This letter had been folded
up and slipped between the pages of a children's book called
The Little House. I knew that book. Jackie had loved it. It
was a story about a country cottage that slowly becomes

swallowed up by the city. Into its green, open meadow comes a road, then cars, soon a train and skyscrapers. In the end, someone lifts the cottage onto a truck and hauls it back out to the country to start a new life away from the noise and the rush of the city—just like the house I had seen when I was thirteen years old, traveling north to the Boundary Waters. Farther down in the newspaper article, Peg was quoted as saying that there were a great many stories that had tempted her, but that the combination of the dog's story and the picture book had swayed her. "I've never sold a house before," she said, "and I enjoyed the process enormously. I will leave here knowing that the house I lived in all these years will be in good, loving hands." She would be moving in two months' time, the article concluded, to a retirement home near her daughter in Berkeley.

I folded up the newspaper and made a note to myself to call the movers to come set my piano upright on its legs.

~

I never bought the enormous pen and ink drawing of a tree that I saw in Portland, Oregon, when I was twenty-three, but I feel as if I've lived with that piece of art my entire life. I can close my eyes and see the whole picture—the subtle shading, the surprising scale, the whiteness of the white where it peeks out from underneath each leaf. I love that painting. The same is true of the bungalow. It's not mine. I spent a grand total of about half an hour in it, but I love it all the same. I love that there exists a house with red walls and old wood floors and a fireplace made of Catalina tile, where a woman who loved her husband and her dogs once lived. In the weeks after the house was sold, I would sometimes drive down Pepper Tree Lane just to look at it again and re-assure myself that it was there.

$\mathcal{T}$UESDAY

In the last week of January, on a day that was cloudless and crystal clear, I drove down to Starbucks in Redondo Village. I love the smell of coffee, the whole idea of it—the hot cup in your hand, the cheerful way you buzz through the day after you've enjoyed it—but I can't drink it; it keeps me awake at night. And I'm an infinitely better human being when I sleep well, so I try to avoid coffee. On that day, however, I was doing revisions on the Chuck Williams piece, and at the same time I was trying to finish a draft for an article about a couple who had designed all the fabric for California Pizza Kitchen restaurants. I needed help to get through the day.

I was standing in line at the counter trying to make sense of the vast number of choices before me, when I heard Peg Torrey place an order. I looked up and saw her standing there, a few places ahead of me.

"I tried to get your house," I said.

She smiled, and it was then I realized that she probably heard that statement several times a day. "What was your reason?" she asked. "It turns out there are only a handful, really, or at least only a handful people confess to."

"The house my husband and I were building was haunted."

Peg looked at as if she could see straight through me. "I haven't heard that one," she said. "You had a ghost?"

"Sort of. We had fear, we had tension. We had our own mortality. They rub off on a house, I think. They stay in the wood and seep through the floors."

Peg looked at me in a way that made me nervous. "That's exactly what I felt about my bungalow, only it was love and joy and the goodness of my husband that seeped through. He was a very good man."

"It sounds like it," I said. "I heard you talk about him on TV."

She smiled again, paid for her coffee, and went outside to sit in the sun. It took me forever to get my cappuccino but when I walked outside, Peg was still sitting in the sun, like a cat at rest.

I smiled at her.

"I was wondering," she said. "What you did with the haunted house."

"We're living in it," I said, "keeping the ghosts at bay. Your house changed everything for us."

"You sent your husband's letters," Peg said.

I wasn't, somehow, surprised by this revelation—that Peg Torrey had read what I had delivered on Christmas Day. "That's right," I said.

"I kept those letters in a shoebox on my bedside table," Peg explained. "I put all my favorites in there."

"I loved your house," I said, "and I loved that you held the contest. I'm glad it turned out so well for you." I hesitated, then turned to leave, as if the conversation were over.

"Would you like to come by?" Peg asked.

It took me a moment to process what she was asking. "Right now?" I asked.

She nodded, waving her hand over her little wrought iron table and the empty coffee cup. "I was just about to walk home. I'd love the company."

∽

I accompanied Peg back to her house on foot. It was about a ten-minute walk along the water, then the half block in. To this day, I don't remember taking that walk. I don't remember if we stopped at the stop signs, if the birds were singing or the waves were pounding. One minute, I was going to Starbucks because I could barely keep my eyes open, and the next minute, I was standing at the door of Peg Torrey's house as she fumbled for her key.

She led me into the dining room, where boxes were stacked along the walls and behind the long side of the big pine table. I turned and pointed toward the mantel, which was swept clean of all its decorations. "You had two mice bookends," I said, remembering. "My grandmother used to have the same set. I loved to play with them. One year when I went to visit, my grandma had a copy of *My Antonia* propped up by the mice. I was too old to pretend the mice could talk and eat bits of cheese, but I still wanted them near me so I put them on the coffee table while I read Willa Cather."

Peg threw her head back and laughed. I could see her teeth, worn down on the tops, yellow, filled with silver. "Did your grandmother have the pig?" she asked.

"No pigs," I said.

"Come this way," Peg said, and just like with Manon at the lingerie store when she asked me to try on the chocolate-colored bra, I felt powerless not to follow. We walked down the hallway where the mounted board games had hung, and into the master bedroom. This was a place I hadn't seen during the open house. It wasn't a big room, but the walls were painted New Mexican turquoise, which made it seem like a little jewel. All the furniture in the room was a rich, dark brown, except for a chair in the corner upholstered in a wild, bright chintz, with dark brown piping.

Peg closed the door behind us, and I felt my heart begin to beat faster, as if there were some kind of danger at hand. She pointed, and there, behind the door, was a little brass pig sitting on a doorstop, with his snout pushed out and his tail curled up behind him. His ears sprung out from his head just like the ears on the mice.

"I found the pig first," Peg explained, "at a bookstore in Aspen, Colorado. This was only about ten years ago. Harry was there for a medical conference. I was so taken with the pig, that I had to bring him home. Harry gave me the mice the next year for Christmas, though he never told me where they came from. It was one of the nicest presents he ever gave me." I could see in her smile the years of gifts she and her husband must have exchanged—years and years of getting it right and getting it wrong and every so often getting it so precisely that the gift in question made the other person's soul sing.

"The nicest present my husband ever gave me," I said, "was a CD player. One of those portable ones with the earphones. It was two weeks before Christmas and I was scheduled for a mastectomy. I wore out this one CD of Christmas carols by Manheim Steamroller. It was better than morphine."

"You beat the cancer?" Peg asked.

I'd never thought of it that way—that I did anything other than what the doctors told me to do. I showed up for appointments, I took the pills they prescribed. "Yes," I said, "I guess I did. I'm just past the five-year mark."

She clapped her hands together with delight. "That's wonderful!" she said, and then a shadow passed over her face. "If Harry were still alive," she said, "I'd tell him that story tonight. I'd tell him how I met you at the coffee shop and how you talked about your house being haunted and then I'd tell him that you'd just celebrated five years being free of cancer. He would have loved it."

"I'm sorry for your loss," I said.

"There's not a day that I don't miss him," she said. "I imagine it will always be so."

~

I drove along the beach, then along the cliffs and past Portuguese Bend, where the road rippled like corrugated steel from an earthquake fault that ran straight out into the sea. Clouds shrouded Catalina Island and the water was clouded with churned-up sand. From the road you could look down and see the houses Rick was framing, rising in a row along the bright green of the seventh tee. Stacks of red clay tile were piled on each roof waiting to be cemented in place.

I turned in on the main drive and wound past the clubhouse. I drove onto freshly black-topped road, and I stopped in front of the first of the new houses, just behind Rick's truck. Rick looked up from the piece of plywood on which he was drawing a sketch. The two men who were standing at the tailgate looked up as well.

"Hey," he said, walking over to my side of the car. "What's going on?" He was curious about what I was doing at his work site, but there was a heaviness to his curiosity—as if he feared I had shown up to deliver bad news, something to do with someone dying or someone being sick.

"I wondered if you'd like to go to lunch," I said.

"What's the occasion?" he asked, still trying to measure the situation.

"No occasion," I said. "I was just thinking about you and thought it might be nice."

He looked at his clipboard and hesitated. Perhaps he was trying to decide if I was telling the truth—that there was nothing wrong or nothing at stake.

"Sure," he finally said. "I'll be ready in a minute."

TUESDAY

Six Months Later

Six months after the sale of the bungalow, I took a detour down Pepper Tree Lane on my way home from the dry cleaner when I saw it: a hole, a bruise, a gaping expanse of dirt where the bungalow had stood. There was a large gray Dumpster on the driveway and a chain-link fence around the perimeter of the property. The eucalyptus trees still stood in stately order along the back fence, and lemons hung off the branches of the trees along the fence, but the lemon tree where Peg had stood when I first spoke to her was no longer there. The avocado trees were gone, the salvia, the stained glass transom windows, the purple trellis—all of it, gone.

I wondered what had happened to the Catalina tile on the fireplace. Had someone bothered to save it, or had it been crushed by an indiscriminate bulldozer and buried in some landfill along with the old copper pipes and the chunks of cement foundation? Some worm would be pleased to come across those subtle shades and intricate patterns.

I pulled the car up on the opposite side of the street and sat there deciding whether or not to cry. There are times when you can do that. You can decide whether or not to step over the edge of your emotion. I wanted to cry, and so I allowed myself to do it. I blinked, and puckered my mouth, and tears streamed down my cheeks.

⌒

When Rick came home that night, he asked if I was OK. He asked three separate times before I finally told him about the bungalow. He nodded, but he didn't express any shock or even surprise. Later that night, when we were in bed and it was dark, I discovered why.

"They asked me to bid on it," he said.

I breathed in and out, in and out, just waiting to see what he might say.

"They came in, just like anyone else—they'd been referred by a client, they'd seen my work. They wanted a three-car garage, a granite island. The wife had a photo from *Sunset* magazine. I started sketching ideas, and I swear to you, April, all I could think about was that bungalow. I skewed the sink in the kitchen just the way the bungalow had it, and I sketched a fireplace just like the one in that front room. Of course the house in the magazine had been built on a half-acre lot, which is nonexistent in the South Bay, and the wife didn't like my orientation. So I asked them if I could take a look at the property. He told me the address, and, well...." He trailed off.

"Why didn't you tell me?" I asked. I had the wild thought that if I had known, I could have stopped it. I could have chained myself to the front door, or set up a platform to camp out in one of the lemon trees. I could have rallied the support of all the people who had tried to get the house, whipped the media into a frenzy.

"I felt like I was part of their shame," Rick said. "I'm the guy with the bulldozer. If not that lot, then some other one."

"You're not like them."

"Yes, I am."

"You absolutely are not."

He shrugged. He didn't buy it.

"What I don't get," I said, "is how they could have done it."

"It's not a registered historic property. There's nothing that would bind them, legally, to preserve it."

"No, I mean, what kind of people could do something like that? What kind of people could win a house like that, accept it, and then tear it down? How can they even sleep at night?"

"I meet them every day," Rick said.

$\mathcal{W}$EDNESDAY

It's a short flight from Los Angeles to Oakland, and an even shorter drive into Berkeley from the airport. Our Daily Bread is located on a busy corner near Cody's bookstore and a shop that sells fresh flowers. All three stores were crammed with customers by the time I arrived. There were lines outside both the flower store and the bakery, and when I took my place in the bakery line I felt like I was in Europe and would be heading to the butcher next for my cut of meat for tonight's dinner.

The bakery smelled of yeast and coffee. The walls

were lined with shelves holding baskets of bread: seven grain, whole wheat, sourdough, sesame. At the front was a case full of éclairs and cookies in the shape of guitars. When I got to the front, I asked for a cinnamon bun and then I asked if I could speak to Sarah. When she came out, she smiled at me.

"I know I know you from somewhere," she said, "I just can't place where."

"I tried to buy your mother's house."

"Right," she said.

"You heard what happened?"

"The neighbors called as soon as the demolition crew showed up, but there was nothing we could do."

"Is your mom OK?"

Sarah pointed to a table by the window. Peg sat there much like she had sat at the Starbucks in Redondo Beach, with a cup of coffee and the paper spread out in front of her.

"May I?" I asked, gesturing toward the table.

"Go right ahead," she said. She wiped her hands on her apron and went back to the kitchen.

I walked over to the table with my cinnamon bun. "May I join you?" I asked.

Peg startled, then looked at me in almost exactly the same way her daughter had a minute before. "You look familiar," she said.

I smiled. "I tried to buy your house. You showed me the mouse bookends."

"Ah," she said. "You're the one with the haunted house."

I laughed. "Yes," I said. "That's me. Do you mind if I join you?"

"Not at all," she said.

I sat down and set my cinnamon bun in front of me. It was piled with pecans, dripping with syrup. "I saw what they did to your house," I said, "and I wanted to say that I was sorry."

"You know what upset me the most?" she said. "It wasn't so much what they did as it was the fact that I judged them so wrong. They weren't who I thought they were. They weren't anything close to who I thought they were. You'd think after seventy-eight years of life I'd be able to accurately judge another human being. I got it completely wrong."

"That would be very upsetting," I said.

She shook her head. "Yes and no. I got what I wanted from the sale of the house."

"What was that?" I asked, thinking of all the gifts that people brought her—the food and the wine, the toffee and the little lemon tree.

"The will to keep living without Harry."

I breathed once, then twice, waiting to see if she'd go on.

"On his last Thanksgiving, we wheeled Harry up to the head of the table," Peg began, "but he didn't eat a single bite of anything, not even Sarah's pumpkin cheesecake. Everyone else just thought the obvious— that he was sick and tired—but I could see from the tilt of his chin and the set of his eye that his not playing and his not eating had a kind of defiance to it that hadn't been there in the previous months.

"'So you're not eating, then?' I asked him later that night. I knew what he was up to. You can't be married to an oncologist for almost fifty years and not know. He nodded in answer to my question.

" 'How long do you figure it will take?' I asked.

" 'A week, maybe ten days,' he said.

"My throat constricted with panic, sadness and a strange gratefulness at his ability to know himself so well and to share himself in such a clear, straightforward way with me.

" 'I wish I could come with you,' I whispered.

"And do you know what he said to me? 'You know I'll be waiting for you.'

"Well, I took him at his word: *You know I'll be waiting for you.* I took him to mean that he would be *waiting*—as if at an airport, or in the lobby of a theater where we had tickets to see a show. Waiting, as if he'd be glancing down at his watch, looking down the street at each car that came, scanning the crowd on the sidewalk for my face. I could feel the weight of all that waiting. I could feel it as if it were a physical reality.

"There had been a lot of death in that house. There were the dogs, of course, and the goldfish and the hamsters, and the big pine tree in the back corner that fell during the Santa Ana winds one year and knocked out the electricity in the entire neighborhood. My life as a young wife died in that house, and my life as a mother of little girls, and finally my life as a married woman. It would have been fitting to die there, for good, among all those endings that had made up our life. I tried. It was easy enough for the widow of an oncologist to get pills. Who, after all, would expect me to be sleeping? I tried. But I simply couldn't do it."

I looked across the bakery table and made some sort of sound in response—a kind of gasp or a sigh.

"He told me he would be waiting for me," Peg said, "but selling the house taught me that it was a different kind of waiting altogether. He's not waiting for me to die. He's waiting for me to finish living."

$\mathcal{E}$PILOGUE

Jackie got her driver's license in May. Her scores, on both the written test and the driving test, were perfect. For weeks before the big birthday, I tried to talk myself into getting her a dog. I looked up dogs on the Internet— dogs from breeders and dogs from the pound, dogs that you could show and dogs that just wanted a warm place to lay their heads at night. Finally, in April, I borrowed a dog for four days, a neighbor's mutt named Bo. I put his food and water dish by the refrigerator and his pillow in Jackie's room, at the foot of her bed. The two days that

Jackie was at school were horrible. Bo sat beside my chair in my office waiting for an opportunity to persuade me to play with him. There I was, looking up research on the psychology of gift-giving, trying to figure out what to say about the five reasons we give, for a holiday article that would be in next December's *Ladies' Home Journal*, and there was Bo, panting at my side, all but saying, "Play with me! Play with me!" When I went out to the grocery store, he whimpered. When I came home, he had piddled on the kitchen floor. Jackie played with him a little bit when she came home from school, then closed her door so she could get her homework done in peace.

We walked Bo right before bedtime, all the way to the end of the street, so I expected him to sleep through the night. In the middle of the night, however, I was awakened by his incessant barking. I waited for Jackie to get up, but she didn't budge. Rick seemed not to hear a thing. Bo was standing in the front hallway, barking furiously at the night. I peered out the window—and saw that I had left my car lights on. I was reminded of a story I once read in the paper about a woman in Florida with a Seeing Eye dog. One day, when the woman wanted to leave the house to do an errand, the dog refused to go. He would not let her put his leash on and would not move toward the door. He barked and barked, and finally, the woman gave up. It was later revealed that an alligator had been sunning itself on the front walk; the dog had saved the woman's life.

Forcing Bo to stay back with one foot, I slipped out and turned off my headlights. I slipped back inside and knelt down to thank Bo for helping me. He hadn't exactly saved my life, but he saved me from having to jump my car, and he'd saved me from having to pretend anymore that I could tolerate a dog. I tried to send him back to his pillow in Jackie's room. He insisted on following me to my bedroom, and, I feel certain, he would have slept on my pillow had I allowed it. Instead, he slept curled at the foot of the bed. I, on the other hand, never really went back to sleep, and when it was time for Bo to go home, I was elated to be free. Whenever I saw him in the neighborhood after that, I would stop and rub him behind his floppy ears.

When Jackie heard that the dog experiment had failed, she grew very quiet. For nearly three days, she hardly spoke. She was more devastated, it seemed, than she had been when Max broke up with her. I checked her e-mail once, just to make sure she was OK. She'd written a note to her friend Alyssa:

My mom hated having Bo here. She hates dogs. I think it's because she can't stand the idea of unconditional love. She can't give it and she can't take it, either. I can't wait to get out of this house.

I have entertained the thought that Jackie found out I was reading her e-mail and wrote that note on purpose to teach me a lesson. The words might as well be etched on the backs of my corneas. I can see them even when I close my eyes. I like to think they're no longer true.

～

Under my beautiful Italian range hood, on the six-burner Wolf stove, I learned how to make chicken tamales with meat that has simmered in a mild tomatillo sauce. I peel the papery skin off the tomatillos by hand, and throw them in the pot with the chicken. After a few hours, the whole house smells good. Lucy tells me that this is the way every house smells in Cuernavaca, Mexico, her family's hometown; to her, it's the exact essence of home. In exchange for her teaching me about tamales, I am teaching her how to play the piano. She happened to come by on the day the movers set up my grandmother's Bösendorfer beneath the big picture window in the living room. She knocked on the door just as the last leg was being screwed down.

"Come in," I said. "Come in and hear this grand piano!"

I paid the movers, then pulled up the black padded bench and played the first phrase of my old favorite Two-Part Invention. It sounded horrible. The keys were grossly out of tune, but I kept playing.

Lucy sat on the edge of the couch and listened—a little audience of one. I could see the look on her face, that look of being overwhelmed by music for the first time.

"Have you ever heard Bach?" I asked.

"What's Bach?" she asked.

"Johann Sebastian Bach. The composer. He wrote the music."

"It makes me sad, this music."

"That's what he wanted."

"To make people sad?"

"Sometimes it feels good to feel sad," I explained.

"Have you ever played the piano?" I asked Lucy.

"This woman, I clean her house and she has a piano."

"Come sit down," I urged.

"No, no," she said.

"You won't hurt it," I said. She came and perched the edge of the little bench.

"This is middle C," I said, pointing to the key. "It's the note where everything else begins. Try it."

She pressed the key, and the note sounded flat from the months in storage.

"Now do this," I said to Lucy. I positioned her fingers so that she could play an open chord. She played the three notes and looked at me, thrilled.

"Would you like to learn how to play?"

"There are too many keys."

"You can start with just three, then go to eight. It's not hard. I'll teach you."

My house is just wallboard and wood. It won't save me, I'm certain of that. But my husband built this house for me, and for Jackie, and for himself, and it's an awfully nice place to be when the sun lowers itself into the ocean and the sky glows orange all the way from Catalina to Malibu. The pelicans fly low over the water in these perfect V's. They're very big birds, and they skim the water with amazing precision. We sit and watch the show, in awe of the color and the space and the black specks they make on the horizon. On nights like that, I feel like I'm at the helm of a boat that's making its way across the sea. I wouldn't say that I feel in charge, but I feel good.

I feel very good.

**FOURTEEN CONVERSATION STARTERS FOR
HOME SEEKERS, BREAST CANCER SURVIVORS,
SHOE LOVERS AND OTHERS WHO MAY WANT
TO DISCUSS THIS BOOK WITH THEIR FRIENDS**
PLUS
Two Behind-the-Scenes Moments from the Author

1. Have you ever fallen in love at first sight with anything or anyone—a person, a dress, a dog or a house? Tell the story of how you fell…and how you landed.

2. Did you have a great tree house as a child? Great windows in your bedroom? A great place to read? Describe the best thing about your childhood home and explain how it is reflected in your current home.

3. Have you, like April and the woman in the Kate Spade pumps, ever left behind a great pair of shoes—or a person, a dress, a dog or a house? Why did you do it?

4. April celebrates her five-year cancer-free anniversary with a Subway sandwich and a bag of chips. If you or someone you love is a breast cancer survivor or a survivor of any

other kind of disease, disorder or disappointment, are you going to celebrate the next big anniversary of being alive—or would you rather let it quietly come and go?

5. Have you ever read letters (or emails) you knew weren't yours to read? Were you sorry you did? Would you do it again?

6. If you've ever lived in a house that had a long history, do you ever think about the people who lived there before you? Do you believe your house has gained—or lost—something by the presence of those other people?

7. April, Rick and Jackie buy a really pathetic Christmas tree from Target—but they would each, no doubt, remember that tree on every holiday for the rest of their lives. Do you have any family holiday traditions in which a less-than-stellar moment is remembered or celebrated?

8. Peg says the mice bookends were the best present Harry ever gave her. April mentions a CD from Rick. What's the best present your beloved has given you? What's the best present you've ever given?

9. Peg met Harry when she accidentally ran over his dog. Do you know anyone whose love was forged through some kind of tragedy?

10. April is healed by a variety of strangers throughout the story, including the nicely dressed woman in the Subway store, the shopkeeper who sells her the Buddha and the shopkeeper who sells her the lingerie. What's the last meaningful encounter you experienced with a stranger?

11. The energy healer tells April she should forgive Rick for loving her so well. Is there something good—or *someone* good or some good part of yourself—that it might serve you well to stop doubting?

12. What's the craziest thing you've ever heard someone do in order to buy or sell a house? If you think your story takes the cake, send it to me at jennie.nash@gmail.com; I'm collecting these tales on my website.

13. April's definition of home skips all over the map throughout this story. What about your own definition of home? How has it changed as you've aged and grown? Where and when do you feel most at home?

14. April's thoughts about mortality lead her to ponder the various legacies a person can leave behind—a sauté pan, a clothing boutique with a conscience, a house full of memories, a house full of air. What kind of legacy do you want to leave behind?

In the middle 2000s, during one of Southern California's frenzied housing booms, my husband and I were looking to trade our Los Angeles starter home for something bigger, better and snazzier, because we thought this was an inalienable right. After two years of searching for a house that we liked that we could afford, our Realtor called from the sidewalk in front of a house about a mile away. It was, she explained, the deal of the century—a good house on a great piece of property in a prime part of town, priced slightly below market value. I jumped in the car and sped over to meet her. She was standing with a crowd of people in the front yard. I recognized several friends of ours in the mix—friends I knew to be looking for houses, too. My husband and I made a bid, but by the end of the day, the price of the house had skyrocketed out of our reach.

In the weeks that followed, I heard a rumor that the house had been purchased for $100,000 over the asking price by a Realtor who had illegally bid against his own client. I found myself wondering about him from time to time, and about all the other people who had bid on that house—what their stories were, and what they had gained and lost. A few months later, I climbed onto a yellow school bus to chaperone a school field trip and took a seat next to the man who had purchased the house. "You don't know me," I said, "but you bought the house I wanted."

He turned to face me. "I actually do know you," he confessed. "My wife had cancer, too." I had written a book about my experiences with cancer, and sometimes forgot that anyone outside my family had read it; I was completely disarmed.

He smiled. "So do you hate me?" he asked.

"I don't *hate* you," I said, "but I've thought a lot about what happened with that house."

"My wife wanted a home where she could live and a home where she could die," he explained. "She decided that was the house and I would have done anything to get it."

I knew in that instant that I would write a story about a man, a woman and a marriage, and the fierce feelings we bring to the search for home.

My husband and I ended up abandoning our search for a new house and decided to remodel instead. I wrote *The Last Beach Bungalow* while the walls came down around us. April has a much cooler house than I do and a *way* better view, but I had a better five-year cancer-free celebration: I took a sunrise walk through a seaside labyrinth and threw a painting party on the concrete subfloor of our new living room.

BEHIND THE SCENES MOMENT #2:
A REAL-LIFE CONTEST TO WIN A HOUSE

There was an actual essay contest held to win a multimillion dollar home in a town not far from mine. This wasn't a fundraising raffle for a nonprofit organization; it was a contest put on by an individual. Each person who sent in an essay about why they wanted to live in this house had to pay a fee of about $140. Thousands of people entered, and there was a great deal of interest in the outcome. What could one person say that would be somehow better than what thousands of other people said? A winner was chosen, but then things got strange. The winner gave the house back to the owner, and it was soon revealed that the winner was actually a distant relative of the owner—a cousin's husband or something like that. The whole thing had been rigged; it was a scam. People who paid their $140 were obviously disappointed—and motivated to take legal action—but I was particularly crushed by the ruse. I loved the idea of someone believing that they could pick out of a crowd the perfect person to inherit their home. I loved the idea of someone being able to win a house on the merits of their story alone. I commandeered the basic elements of the contest, conjured up a wonderful widow to run it, and ended up with the spine of my story.